THE WELL AND OTHER STORIES

THE WELL AND OTHER STORIES

NICK FARAGHER

*Thanks Jacqueline,
a pleasure to sign this
for you. Cheers [signature]*

thistledown press

Thistledown Press Ltd.
633 Main Street, Saskatoon, SK   S7H 0J8
www.thistledownpress.com

Library and Archives Canada Cataloguing in Publication
Faragher, Nick, 1945-
The well and other stories / Nick Faragher.
Short stories.
ISBN 978-1-897235-48-5
I. Title.
PS8611.A71W45 2008   C813.6   C2008-904521-1

Publisher Cataloging-in-Publication Data (U.S.)
(Library of Congress Standards)
Faragher, Nick.
The well and other stories / Nick Faragher.
[197] p. :   cm.
Summary: Psychologically quirky and sometimes darkly engrossing short stories that plunge the reader into the edgy minds of distracted characters. Set in Greece, Italy, the French Alps and Canada's west coast.
ISBN: 978-1-897235-48-5 (pbk.)
1. Short stories, Canadian. 2. Canadian fiction – 21st century.
I. Title.
813.6 dc22   PS3603.A7We   2009

Cover photograph (detail) by Kathy Kaiser
Cover and book design by Jackie Forrie
Printed and bound in Canada

10 9 8 7 6 5 4 3 2 1

| Canada Council for the Arts | Conseil des Arts du Canada | | Canadian Heritage | Patrimoine canadien |

Thistledown Press gratefully acknowledges the financial assistance of the Canada Council for the Arts, the Saskatchewan Arts Board, and the Government of Canada through the Book Publishing Industry Development Program for its publishing program.

THE WELL AND OTHER STORIES

For my children, Oscar, Hugo, Brodie, Bayley, Annie and Gracie, and The North Shore Connexions Society, staff and volunteers who enable my dear son, Hugo to live his life fully.

Contents

La Piazzo del Cignois   11

The Promising Artist   28

Knickers   46

A Wee Bit of Fun   68

The Well   88

Birds for Breakfast   129

The Watch Seller   147

A Place To Hang Out   168

La Piazzo del Cignois

IN MILAN, THERE WAS ALWAYS THE NOISE and earth smell of construction and the taste of grit in the air, but not in the square named, interestingly, Piazzo del Cignois. Piazzo del Cignois was one of the smaller squares in the city, away from the centre with its wide and important spaces where beautiful women strolled in twos and threes by the shops in the *gallerias*. The air in the square was fragrant with the scent of blossoms from forty cherry trees, and the old grey stones of the square were softened by their dying, pink petals. The noise of the city was muted. The clamour of traffic, the thump of pile drivers and the clank of heavy equipment sounded like foghorns on a misty morning on the coast, not unheard but not obtrusive, a reminder of another and distant world.

Piazzo del Cignois was a mix of residential and unassuming commercial activity. The latter, accountants and designers and the like, announced their presence discreetly by way of small brass plaques by their front doors. The more visible exceptions were a corner wine bar, a trattoria on the diametrically opposed corner and a small, self-effacing hotel, its presence so muted that it was barely distinguishable from an accountant's practice on its west side and a private residence on its east.

At the centre of the square was a circular pool surrounded by a low, broad, stone wall. Here, a person might sit comfortably, sipping coffee bought from the trattoria, and reading the morning paper, or make a wish and toss another coin into the flat water and watch it sink quickly to the dark green bottom where the tolls for a thousand other forgotten and cheaply bought wishes lay. In the middle of the pool stood the algae-striated statue of a nude woman. She was proffering a stone jug from which water bubbled brown over the lip and trickled down her arm and body and back into the pool with scarcely a ripple.

Two things stood out on the nearly indisguishable hotel: the rather larger brass plate next to the front door which read Hotel de Bruno, and the distinctive staircase leading up to the front door. Most of the residences had two or three front steps but Bruno's, set a little higher and a little further back from the blossom-strewn flagstones of the square, had eight. Originally, there had been no handrail, but when the building had been converted into a commercial property city by-laws required that one be installed. Bruno had put in a curved brass rail supported on either side by hollow brass tubes, sunk to different depths in the ground at the side of the staircase. It smacked a little of ostentation, although Bruno was not an ostentatious man.

On the opposite side of the square a young boy of thirteen or so, the son of the owner of the trattoria, placed a cup of cappuccino on the wrought iron table at which a girl was sitting. Perhaps she was not a girl, but a young woman, as much as the boy was clearly a boy. It was mid-afternoon and, although never busy, the square was now in the hollow quiet of siesta time with only the young woman, the boy, and a slender pale-grey cat occupying it. Taking a sip of coffee, the girl placed the cup back in the saucer and crossing her brown legs leaned back in the chair, her long, dark hair hanging in a loosely-tied scallop behind the graceful curve of her neck. She watched the cat carefully pick its way through the thin shadows hemming the buildings on the western side and occasionally pause at some sound or movement, looking around with the solemn wariness of a predator. Now it paused again, this time longer. Following its gaze, the girl, Helen, saw a boy come into the square from the corner where the wine store stood.

Walking with purpose, his eyes turned downwards, the boy approached the small hotel which the girl had left that morning. On reaching the steps, the boy stopped. He looked around quickly, hesitated a moment or two as his gaze passed over the spot where the girl was sitting, then stepping onto the border at the side of the steps, he retrieved from his pocket two short metal rods that twinkled briefly in the sunshine. He knelt briefly and reached out, appearing to touch the base of the steps as though in homage, then came quickly to his feet. His hands and arms moving in a blur, he struck out at the brass uprights supporting the handrail.

As the first sound — a note — sang out across the square, the grey cat fled and a host of roosting pigeons clattered noisily away across the fronts of the quiet buildings. The girl smiled; she recognized the music at once — Bach. A couple of shutters opened in the houses surrounding the square and she knew that she was not the only listener. The young man played without interruption for several minutes until, with the ghost of the last note still ringing in the air, he returned the two metal rods to his pocket. To Helen's surprise, and secret delight, he walked across the square toward the small circular table where she was sitting, or at least toward the trattoria which stood behind her.

Helen could not ignore him as he passed, and looking up she said, "*Signore, bellissimo, bella musica.*"

The young man paused mid-stride and looked down at her, "*Grazie, Signorina, non era niente.*"

"*No, non era niente, era cosi bella,*" Helen repeated.

The young man appeared to consider his options for a moment, before suddenly resting his hand on the back of the chair opposite her, "*Signorina, permesso?*"

What could she say? She was intrigued and enchanted, flattered and young. She smiled her permission.

The young man sat in the chair, leaned back, crossed his legs, and looked across at her. "You are English?" he said smiling.

She should have been offended; she was rather proud of her mastery of the rhythm of the language. Even though she would be the first to admit that she was far from fluent, she had thought that her Italian was good enough that with her dark complexion and brown eyes she might, initially at least, be mistaken for a native. Humbled she asked, "My accent is so bad?"

The young man's smile widened. "Not bad *Signorina,* but recognizable and also beautiful . . . as you are."

She laughed at that, although she knew it was true. Every Italian man she had ever met had told her that. It was, she thought, built into the genetic code of Italian men that they must flatter young women while they still honestly could, before the women became fat from too much time spent in *patisseries,* and before they reached the age where the only

14

flattery came from gigolos who, with their youth, noble looks and hard virility, sought to benefit.

"What is beautiful is what you just did, beautiful and amazing," Helen said, trading compliment for compliment.

The young man smiled modestly. "It was a little . . . *bruto* I think, but if I made some likeness to music and it pleased you, then I am happy." After saying this, he spoke quickly, almost sternly to the boy who had stepped out from the doorway of the trattoria.

"Posso avero un Campari."

"You are far too modest," the girl said, "you made those railings, those pipes sing, and not some little jingle, but Bach. You are a musician?"

"Alas, no, I am only a plumber. I work with pipes," the young man replied, casting his eyes downwards.

Helen thought his humility beautiful, but a plumber? To cover her dismay, the girl smiled briefly and took another sip of her coffee. "I play piano. I play quite well, but I could not do what you just did on that railing. You are a musician," she said emphatically. She noticed then that the cat had returned and was sitting on the eastern side of the square, head up, with its throat exposed, basking in the afternoon sunshine. The pigeons had also returned and were cluttering the ledges of the buildings, chuckling softly to one another. The boy from the trattoria walked over to the table and, placing a glass of Campari in front of the young man, smiled sadly, turned, and trailed back to the store.

"I wonder why he seems so sad?" she asked, without expecting an answer.

"It is clear he is only a boy, but he has dreams and wonders if one day he will have his own trattoria and sit with such a beauty," said the young man.

Helen knew of course that his flattery was calculated, but allowed herself to revel in it nonetheless. She felt herself flush slightly.

The young man leaned forward and spread his hands, palms up, on the table. The girl examined them; they were strong and brown. When she looked up, she found herself pierced by his dark brown gaze and she felt her heart jump. He was what every English girl expected an Italian man might be: his hair dark and curly, a day's growth of dark beard, outrageously and sensuously good looking with a strong Roman nose, full lips, cleft chin, and a masculine confidence that caused a flood of excitement to run through her. She noticed the beads of sweat on his chest hair from the exertion of his performance in the heat of the afternoon.

"Place your hands in mine, *Signorina*. I will tell you about yourself." He spoke softly, but with such firmness and authority that she felt compelled to obey. She placed her own small, paler hands in his, and felt them enveloped in his heat.

"You are eighteen, no, nineteen years of age and you are . . . you have come here to Italy with another, but not a lover I think . . . although you have known a lover, of course. How could you not have done — such beauty does not pass unnoticed among men . . . your English would have to be a nation of donkeys for it to be otherwise." The girl blushed again when he said this, "You have come . . ." he continued, "with . . . ah, your parents."

Helen tried not to show surprise, but it was true. She had come here with her parents just four days ago, partly to celebrate her nineteenth birthday last week, and partly at her mother's insistence to help her get over the break-up she had just had with her childhood sweetheart. It had come about because she had gone off to university, while he hadn't. Her mother had assured her that he had just been a stage, and that had led to an awful row. However, deep down, she had recognized that her mother was probably right, that she was growing beyond her first serious boyfriend. Helen looked at the young man before her and chafed at being caught out — a girl masquerading as a woman, here with her parents! But she was also impressed and fascinated and said only "Go on," thus acknowledging the accuracy of his reading of her.

"You have suffered some recent pain of the heart I find, but you are very young and strong, and you have many loves in your future," said the young man smiling.

"Well I don't know about that," she answered quickly, but strangely happy she wondered if the 'strong' would come to her soon and if letting go of her boyfriend was part of it.

"Ah, but I do," said the young man. "With beauty must go love and some pain perhaps, but more love than pain. Sometimes tragedy, it is true — but not in your case."

"How do you know all this?" Helen asked, now believing every word.

The the young man, looked up sharply, "Forgive me beautiful girl, I must go. Forgive me." With that, and a quick clasp of her hand, he rose from the table and turned to go.

She sat for a moment in disbelief until she stuttered from the dumbness of her confusion, "But wait, I don't even know . . . "

"Raphael," called out the boy. "I will be here tomorrow."

"Raphael who?" she called.

But he didn't turn back, and continued to stride quickly across the square, the way he had come.

The young woman lingered over the remains of her cappuccino. How had he guessed her age so accurately? Most men thought she was in her twenties, and how had he known she had come here with her parents? She wondered if he came here often, but knew that his amazing performance on the hotel railings guaranteed he did. She also knew where she would be coming for coffee at the same time tomorrow. She left a couple of the brightly coloured thousand-lira notes on the table and wandered back across the square and toward the Hotel de Bruno. When she reached the front steps, she paused and looked at the railings supporting the handrail before continuing up and through into the hotel.

"Mum, Dad, you didn't hear him. It was amazing, just with two . . . I don't know, forks or something and he played like he was in a concert hall. I couldn't believe what I heard, I mean he played Bach! From a plumber! You must ask Bruno about him. He must have heard him play before. And he was so good looking, I mean God, I mean *like* a god."

The young woman's mother looked at her husband, and then back at her daughter. "Sweetheart, we are in Italy, the home of romance, of Puccini. It is expected that you will meet an Italian man who, however vaguely, resembles a god. But they are not gods; they are young men with one thing on their minds most of their conscious hours, and I'm not talking about football." Joan Hogan looked again at her husband, "Well, Brian?"

The titular head of the family was a long-suffering man, and had been for the twenty-six years of his marriage. Long inured to his wife's jaundiced view of his gender, he nonetheless recognized that she was probably right on this occasion. He looked across at his daughter, whom he loved dearly, and who reminded him of his wife when she'd been younger — thirty years younger. He looked down at the bowl of pasta in front of him, the gentle shining ivory curves of the tortellini. A suggestion of something erotic stirred — faded memories of a honeymoon. He gave the pasta a stir with his fork and let his gaze travel to the half-full glass of red wine to the side of his plate. Again, the voluptuous curve at the base of the glass hinted at something just beyond his grasp.

"Brian?" his wife prodded.

Brian Hogan wondered about this young man that had so attracted his daughter. "Actually, dear, I was thinking that football is exactly what most young Italian men spend their time thinking about," he said sadly.

"Oh for goodness sake! You know exactly what I mean!" his wife retorted with undisguised irritation, "Our daughter is infatuated with a plumber, an Italian plumber, and you make light of it."

In part to defend herself, and in part to come to the aid of her besieged father, their daughter interjected, "Mother! I'm not infatuated with him. My God! I don't even know him. All I said was that he made the most beautiful music from the railings at the front of our hotel and that he was good looking — which he was, I mean, is."

"Like a god, I believe is how you described him, dear," replied her mother.

"And anyway, what's wrong with being a plumber?" added Helen without conviction.

At 2:30 the following afternoon, Bruno stepped out onto the top step of his small hotel. Bruno was a big man, big in all the ways it is possible to be big, big in height, in girth, in presence. One hundred and twenty kilos, when he had last weighed himself, and that had been some twelve years before.

And if those years spent walking the earth had compressed his spine just a little, his girth and weight had suffered no such diminution. Quite to the contrary, he had had to have his pants let out every year or so and replaced along with his jackets every four years.

Pulling the door closed behind him, Bruno stepped further out into the afternoon sunlight. He surveyed the square below him, the square that had been his home for some years past. He looked across toward the trattoria, but the tables stood empty and forlorn, and only the door standing ajar suggested the possibility of service. He heard the soft pad of footsteps approaching and knew without looking to whom they belonged. When the footsteps stopped in front of him, he shifted his gaze and looked down at the boy.

"You vagabond, are you here again disturbing my guests?"

The young man smiled up at him, "Bruno, I introduce a little magic into their lives, you know I do."

"Magic!" cried Bruno in apparent astonishment. "My young friend, you flatter yourself. You are a fraud, not a magician; there is a difference. To be a magician is to pursue an honourable profession, rooted in history."

The young man looked suitably chastened and his expression, a mask of humility, said, "You are right of course, Bruno. I cannot deny it."

Bruno huffed a little as if to acknowledge the correctness of the admission. Then his countenance abruptly broke into avuncular indulgence.

"But your antics amuse me and anyway this time I think you will lose."

"So," began the young man cautiously, "we are on?"

"Yes, we are on, you thief . . . we are on for 30,000 lira. She is a beauty to be sure and were I perhaps a little less the victim of my appetite, I would take the child to bed myself, rather than you, you sorry rascal, who has nothing to offer but your dishonesty."

The young man grinned broadly, "Sadly, Bruno, I must agree with you: age, pasta, and vino have severely compromised both your looks and your prospects . . . possibly your ability?"

Bruno snapped at him with the white linen cloth he had been holding over his arm, and the boy skipped adroitly back. "As I said, boy. I think with this one, you will not find her so easy, not like that last one, the American girl. Americans are like children; they will believe anything. They should not be out alone. This one she is smart; you are not. She is here, as I told you, with her parents and she is gone the day after tomorrow, back to London, safe from the likes of you."

The young man shook his head, "Bruno, these details are hardly obstacles . . . Forty-eight hours is a desert of time."

Bruno's gaze travelled up and across the boy's shoulder, "Ah," the latter announced without turning around, "Perhaps the object of our discourse has arrived?"

The young woman took a seat at the same table she had occupied the day before. Today, she had walked with her parents for a good part of the morning. They had lunch together at a little restaurant suggested by Bruno, just off via Paulo Sappi. After lunch, in the full heat of the day, her parents conceded the wisdom of the siesta and returned to the hotel. This left the young woman free to go to the trattoria and see if the young man from the day before would once more work his magic on the railings of the hotel steps.

When first entering the square, Helen immediately noticed the young man talking to Bruno. She pretended not to notice and went directly to the handful of tables in front of the trattoria. She had been there only a few moments when the young boy with the sad expression emerged from the shadowed doorway of the trattoria behind her. Although there was no sign of the cat, the birds were there — almost silent, small, fluttering grey ghosts under the eaves of the buildings, with only the occasional soft coo to give them away.

Helen watched the young man as he turned away from Bruno. He looked up quickly, and it was too late to shift her gaze. He smiled briefly and gave a small bow. Then, as yesterday, he knelt briefly by the steps, reached out to touch them, then immediately stood and began to play. It was a piece she didn't recognize.

"It is a popular love song from the South," the voice said in halting and heavily accented American English.

Helen started. She had not heard the boy from the trattoria approach, and anyway, had been quite intently focused on the young man across the square. The boy was standing a short distance behind her and in his hand was a white cloth with which he now began to wipe the tables.

"*Grazie, non so,*" Helen replied, then switching to English added, "You speak very good English. Where did you learn?"

"Movies," said the boy, simply.

"Ah," said the girl, then, "It sounds very . . . melancholy . . . sad."

"My English?" said the boy.

"No! No!" she laughed, "The tune that young man is playing . . . He's very talented."

"Ah," said the boy, "yes, he is very good at what he does. He has a reputation for his talent."

"So, *permesso*, tell me more about the tune, the song," she asked.

The boy was clearly pleased to be able to tell the young woman about the song. "It is about a young man who falls in love with a young and beautiful girl. Her parents do not approve because he is poor. He leaves to make his fortune in the North so he can come back a wealthy man and claim her for his wife."

"Ah," said Helen, "I think every country and every language must have its own version of this story."

"When he comes back it is some years later, but he is now very wealthy and very powerful."

"I think that could be guessed," said the girl.

"Of course she could not wait, he was gone a long time," continued the boy.

"She has married another?" Helen suggested.

"She had stayed single a long time, out of love for the young man, but finally, just a short time before, yes, she had married an older man in the village who is quite rich, but not so rich and powerful like the young man."

"What happens?" she asked.

"The hero, he is distraught and, in his sorrow, he kills her," said the boy.

"That sounds very Italian," Helen smiled at the boy.

"Yes, I think so too," said the boy, "Is very beautiful and very sad."

"Although she didn't deserve to be killed," said the young woman.

"She was very beautiful," said the boy with a shrug.

A few moments later, the last note trembling in the air, the performance was finished. As he had the day before, the young man returned the rods to his pocket and turning, began to walk across the square toward her. The boy from the trattoria smiled his sad smile and returned to the shadowed doorway of the store.

"I told you the boy was in love with you, and who can blame him," said the young man as he put his hand on the back of the chair opposite, the same chair he had occupied yesterday, and again asked her permission, although this time with just his eyebrows.

"Please." Helen gestured at the empty chair. As he sat, she continued, "That was beautiful, but sad. The boy told me the story."

"I played it only for you," said the young man, "for you and my friends the pigeons. Today even they do not fly away, perhaps out of respect for the tragic young couple."

The young woman laughed, "I wanted my parents to come and listen to you play but I think the heat and wine with lunch were too much for them. I think they are probably sleeping, taking siesta."

"Ah, *Signorina*, in Italy siesta is not always for sleeping."

She laughed again, "Perhaps you are right. I know my father thinks that there is something immoral about siesta, that the idea of sleeping during the day is immoral, that only lazy people would sleep when they could be working."

"Ah, yes," said the boy, "I have heard of that peculiar English idea. The idea that there is something noble in work at the expense of everything else, work at the expense of living." The young man paused then and the girl remained silent. "You are beautiful,' he said suddenly, leaning forward with his hands pressed together in front of his lips, his eyes boring into hers so that she blushed and looked away.

"Something tells me you have used that line before," she said, laughing a little awkwardly. He looked slightly pained and she felt guilty and compelled to add, "but thank you."

"In Milano, many people do not take siesta, not like people in the South. I think people here think they are too busy, perhaps too important and that only simple people, country people take siesta. Making money is all people here think about," said the young man.

"You are from the South?" asked the girl.

"*Si*, from a small village close by Naples. I believe it is the most beautiful village in the whole of Italy," said the young man with utter conviction.

"I think siesta is a wonderful custom," said Helen, losing her blush. "If I lived here I think I would take siesta all the time," she added.

"If you lived here, I think I, too, would want, with you, to take siesta all the time," said the young man mischievously.

"You are bad," said the girl smiling.

"I do not think such feelings that I have could possibly be called bad," replied the young man.

In order to divert herself, Helen took another sip of her cappuccino and was aware that her hand was trembling slightly. She replaced the cup in the saucer, then wiped away a thin rim of foamed milk from her upper lip.

"Do you live far from here?" she asked.

"I live close by," said the boy. "I could show you if you would like?"

"I'm leaving tomorrow," said the girl.

"I know, Bruno told me," said the boy.

Helen looked across at the hotel and asked carefully, "What else did Bruno tell you?"

The boy smiled, "That you were here with your parents and this visit to my beautiful country is to celebrate your nineteenth birthday."

Helen tried to look annoyed, but failed, "And so you are not a magician?"

The boy started at her choice of that word, and wondered if she, too, had talked with Bruno.

"I mean clairvoyant," she continued without noticing his alarm, then added, "but that takes nothing away from your music."

Recovered, the boy said, "I have never played so well. I have you to thank. To play for such beauty is an honour for a man."

The girl looked at the young man. She was awed at how complete was his submission to her. She wondered when she might ever be in Milan again. She looked up at the beauty of the old buildings, at the statue of the naked woman rising out of the water, and the fruitful bounty of her body. "How much do you want to make love to me?"

The boy dropped to one knee and took both of her hands in his, "More than life, *Signorina*, more than life."

The next day the girl and her parents left as planned. Bruno and the young man stood on the steps of the hotel and waved as the cab pulled away. Its three occupants waved back. The young man blew a kiss, then clasped his hands to his forehead with great melodrama. Helen smiled and her mother looked at her quizzically.

"Who was that, dear?" she asked in a pointedly neutral tone.

"Oh, Mother, that was just the young man I told you about, the one who played on the railings while you and Daddy were enjoying siesta." Her father coughed abruptly and looked intently out of the window on the other side.

"He seemed to know you." her mother persisted.

"We spent some time together, during the siesta time . . . he's Italian; he's a romantic."

Joan Hogan sniffed, "Dear, do you have the tickets and passports ready?"

"Yes, dear," replied her husband.

Their daughter smiled a secret smile.

Watching the taxi accelerate through a red light, Bruno turned toward his young companion and, speaking in the dialect of the village twenty miles to the north from which they both came, said, "Here you are, boy," and taking his wallet from his back pocket, he pulled out several thousand lira notes. "In so short a time I would not have thought it possible, but I concede defeat."

The boy smiled as he took the money. "She was young and impressionable I confess, but she was a musician also and admired my talent."

"Aghh! Your talent! That is what really hurts, that you should get away with such cheap trickery. It hurts even more that I paid for the system. I swear one day I will pull the plug on you and see how you charm your way out of that."

The boy laughed, "You will never do that, Bruno, you would miss our little sport, speaking of which I have left my CD on your player. May I come and get it?"

"Come, my young friend, we will celebrate your shabby victory with a glass."

The two walked back into the hotel entrance, passing between two small speakers on either side of the doorway. From these speakers, the lyrics of a much-played Italian love song floated out into the square and into the clatter and bustle of a beautiful Milanese morning.

The Promising Artist

FIFTY-SEVEN, FIFTY-EIGHT, FIFTY-NINE . . . SIXTY. Duncan stopped at sixty, his face a rictus of pain and effort. Elbows locked, hands shoulder-width apart and flat on the floor, he pulled his right knee forward, took the weight of his one-hundred-sixty-six pounds on his right leg and, drawing up his left knee, came to a squatting position from which he levered himself to his feet. He'd started the workout routine almost six months ago, in fact, when he thought about it, six months ago to the day. He'd started November first and today was May Day. He liked to finish with push-ups. He exulted in the feeling of strength and power the exercise gave him, the sheer effort of will in overcoming the physical limits the final five or six leverages always required. The routine was half-an-hour long and followed a five-kilometre run that took about the same amount of time. He looked at himself in the long mirror on the front of his closet door. After returning from his run, he'd discarded his spandex running suit and performed his floor exercises naked. His lightly muscled, tanned body glowed with a fine sheen of sweat; his abdominal muscles resembled the dark wet corrugation of a beach above the line of an ebbing tide.

Duncan gazed at his reflection with satisfaction. Even in repose, his penis was a fine organ. He moved his hand to hold it, was proud of its thickness and weight. He continued to hold his penis while he examined the features of his face. Clean cheekbones, a straight, fine-boned nose, and high forehead, in short, a certain nobility of profile. Not for the first time, when examining himself in a mirror, he was reminded of Greco-Roman frescoes depicting the ideal male figures of antiquity. He smiled at the thought, but noticed that the lines and creases that had once hinted at an outdoor recreational life spent squinting into the sun, now hinted simply at the inevitability of ageing. He turned to one side, watching the way his skin tightened across his stomach, but noticed with distaste that the lines in his neck were quite evident. *I'm starting to look like a turkey*, thought Duncan and jutted his jaw a little. The lines flattened, it was true, but now even his posture was turkey-like. *I can hardly walk around like this*, he thought. A glance at his watch alerted him to the fact that it was fifteen minutes before nine; he was meeting Amelia at The Roaster coffee house at nine-thirty.

In the small bathroom of her second-floor corner apartment, Amelia put the finishing touches to her eye shadow, then replaced the brush in its holder. The pink teddy bear with a blue bow, a present from her grandfather when she'd left Calgary for Vancouver, sat watching her. The tag attached to the collar read, in carefully formed letters, "To Pooks with love from Ticky." Amelia let out a long breath but it didn't relieve the tightness in her head. Taking a tall, pink can of hairspray in her left hand, she ran the fingers of her right through her bobbed hair as she fired a couple of bursts of the toxic mist into it.

Looking at herself in the mirror was often a difficult moment for Amelia. On the one hand, she considered herself cute — *how could any man not see that?* she pondered; on the other hand, she couldn't remember a time when she hadn't struggled with her weight. She'd starve herself for weeks and lose a couple of pounds, then put it back on over a weekend. At five-feet five inches, there was no reliable way to conceal an extra thirty pounds, but a good sense of style and her innate ability to dress to make the most of herself, helped. On this morning, she wore a long skirt and a roll-neck sweater believing the combination would have a slimming and lengthening effect. To a degree she was right, but the effect was compromised by the fact that she was overdressed for the warm, spring morning and, already, she could feel the heat in her face.

Amelia had been lucky to get a corner apartment; painting was her passion and she valued natural light. Although only on the second floor, the front wall of her apartment was almost all glass, with no buildings to block the expansive view of English Bay. She would often sit on her small balcony and watch sailboats returning to their moorings in False Creek, or just gaze at the setting sun.

Looking around to make sure she'd forgotten nothing, left nothing switched on that should be off, Amelia took in a long, low, narrow windowsill upon which a collection of assorted pastel-hued, stuffed animals sat, slouched and sprawled. A pretty shawl in muted earth tones was deliberately draped across the back of a contemporary chaise lounge, and on a small, oval table — one of a matched pair — a bowl of dried flowers had been arranged with tender care. At the other end of the chaise, atop the matching table, stood a graceful figurine of a ballerina, an image that was reflected in the

Degas print on the wall beside the door. On the long back wall above a low dresser, hung two oil paintings with the artist's signature, *A. P.* in the bottom right corner. One of the pair was strangely poignant — a little girl in a white dress sitting on a garden swing, another swing hanging empty next to her. The other painting showed a child in the act of placing a pair of pink ballet slippers in the bottom drawer of her dresser. A blue teddy bear lay on the floor next to her knee and the rounded tip of a shoe just visible in the bottom right corner of the painting suggested a parental presence. In fact, the room was steeped in images and icons of fragile, delicate femininity — except of course for Amelia herself.

Off this main living area, a second smaller room functioned as a studio. With glass on the same south-facing front wall, windows continued around to cover half the west-facing wall so that daylight flooded the space from one-and-a-half sides. Stacks of empty frames, boards, and canvasses were propped against one wall, and a collection of bent and twisted tubes of oils, pots of brushes, an umbrella, a broken easel, drawing pads, and a dozen other odds and ends crowded up against the other. Half the floor was covered by a crumpled drop cloth, and in the corner between the windows, a work-in-progress was propped on an easel. Even the most indifferent observer could discern that the same hand had painted both the unfinished work on the easel and the two in the main living area. All three had in common a domestic setting conceived in a dappled, blurry style, as though ambiguity was preferred over reality. The incomplete scene was of a young girl ironing with her back to a half-open doorway through which an old person's fingers clasped the arm of a chair.

"Now where have I put my keys?" Amelia asked herself out loud, and after her cursory inspection of the living area failed to reveal them, she stepped into her bedroom. The errant keys, complete with an attached assortment of toys and fobs, were on the corner of a dresser crammed with tubes, bottles, and small, framed pictures of various family members — including herself at different stages of her life. Keys in hand, Amelia sat down on the small cane stool and looked at the pictures. There was a picture of her and her sister, Tabatha, when they had each earned a First in their respective age divisions at an inter-school gym meet. The picture was Amelia's favourite. How slim they both were, with bodies like boys under their matching Lycra gym suits. Amelia had been twelve when the picture was taken and Tabatha just ten years old. Tabatha was smiling nervously, while Amelia looked very serious. Another picture placed them both on horseback. She remembered the Big T Ranch where it had been taken. A man with a white beard and a crooked smile held the bridle of the horse that Amelia rode. The horse was named Shady and the man was her grandfather who, for reasons that were now quite lost to her, she had always known as Ticky. There was a picture of her mother too, and not for the first time, Amelia noticed how both her mother and Tabatha had the same uncertain smile. It was the eager-to-please smile that a child might have when asked to pose for a photograph by a relative, the sort of smile that robbed the picture of sincerity. There was no picture of her father, a father who'd left them — left her — when she was three. That was when her mother had taken them to live with Grandma and Grandpa out beyond Hundred Mile House.

Amelia raised her eyes and looked at herself in the mirror. She looked at her plump cheeks and the beginnings of a double chin, then again at the picture of her and Tabatha. Her lips trembled and puckered; her features crunched up and she started to cry. Amelia grabbed at a handful of tissues from the box on the dressing table, crushed them to her face, and burying her face in the cloud of white, let out an agonized, tortured cry, her body shaking from the violence of her emotion.

It still happened whenever she thought of Tabatha, even now after all this time. How could she have done it?

It had been a spring day, not unlike this day, and Amelia had returned from school expecting to find Tabatha already home. Not finding her in the main house, she'd guessed she must be down at the barn with the horses, the first place she'd go after dropping her things at the house. That their grandparents weren't home wasn't unusual, they'd probably gone into Hundred Mile. Pushing open the barn door and calling her sister's name, she'd seen her almost at once. Tabatha, in her favourite yellow sweater and the jeans she all but lived in, was standing in the shadow of one of the big uprights that supported the roof. But then Amelia saw she wasn't standing, she was hanging, unmoving, her head over to one side and the red-and-white lunge-line twisted tightly around her neck and looped around the beam above her head. Amelia hadn't understood, not at first. Thinking her little sister was playing some kind of a joke, she had approached her slowly, past the toppled stool. Then the awful, nightmare realization, the silence fractured by screaming, the screaming that was her.

After the emotional storm had passed, Amelia looked again at her image in the glass, her face a blotchy, smeared wreck. She let out a long sigh and, putting the tissues into the waste bin by the side of the dressing table, she reached again for her makeup box.

At nine-forty-two, Duncan arrived at the Roaster for his date with Amelia. "Hi, Amelia, sorry I'm late. Some business I had to take care of."

Amelia's breezy reply failed to mask the relief she felt, "Oh, no, that's okay, I only just got here myself," she lied. Then in an effort to authenticate the lie, added, "I've not even touched my coffee yet." But the untouched coffee was no longer hot, and a telltale slick of cream wrinkled its surface.

Duncan smiled tightly and slid his yellow tinted aviator sunglasses back into his strawberry-blond hair. He lowered himself into the chair opposite with studied languid grace, pausing for just a moment as he caught sight of his reflection in the dark glass. "I thought we might have coffee, but I see you've already . . . anyway, and then I want to take you to a little exhibition, a promising young painter. Nice review in the *Georgia Strait*—basically immature stuff but if one has an eye for promising talent . . . and, of course the prices are, well . . . "

"Yes, I'd love to, that sounds . . . actually—" Amelia began.

"Good, good," Duncan cut in. "Then let's go. You never know. There might be something that catches my eye and as you paint a bit yourself, your opinion would be . . . well . . . could be useful." He signalled for the waitress and, while they waited, he studied Amelia across the small table. He'd always considered thinness in women next to godliness, but he didn't believe in God, so that left only thinness. *She's certainly packing a few extra pounds,* he told himself.

They'd met through a telephone introduction agency. He'd listened to the free-to-listen-to ads for six months before taking the plunge into what was called the "Live-Time

Café." It had taken him several times to hone his little blurb to his satisfaction.

"Hi, ladies, my name is Duncan. I'm tall, athletic, and have been told I look like Robert Redford. I'm a successful and financially secure professional, and I'm looking for an attractive woman in her twenties who enjoys fine dining, off-the-wall lifestyle, the arts, and sex."

He figured that had all the bases covered; he liked the "off-the-wall" bit. On reflection, he decided that "sex" was a bit blunt and so re-recorded it one more time with "romantic evenings" substituting for sex. But that, of course, was a cliché. So, another recording with "passionate evenings" followed, and that, he felt, would have to do. He knew it didn't describe him exactly, but it was close enough. He wasn't going to do it a seventh time. His job as assistant manager at the Cypress branch of the Royal Bank might not strictly qualify him as a professional, but it was close enough. While nobody had actually suggested to him that he resembled Robert Redford, he'd certainly noted more than a passing likeness — when the actor was much younger, of course. In fact, when he listened back to it, he wondered why he was advertising at all — the guy was obviously a winner. That's when he decided to add, "Too busy to go the conventional route," and made yet one more recording.

He thought again about Amelia's ad. Really, it wasn't even close. She'd described herself as "an artistic, full-figured, fun-loving, blue-eyed, blonde professional who enjoys art, the classics, cabernet-sauvignon, and cosy evenings." She should have been a perfect match, but full-figured was an under-statement, and the rest, well who knew? She was certainly not the little blue-eyed, blonde nymphet that had danced across his mind. He'd assumed that full-figured was code for big breasts — but only big breasts — not big everything else. If she had said she was thirty pounds overweight, he'd have moved right along. Artistic? What at, cooking? However, he hadn't known that when they'd first chatted over the agency link. He'd liked the sound of her voice, which was warm and feminine, and the way she listened to him without interrupting.

They'd arranged, for their first date, to meet outside The Paragon Theatre on Broadway to see the movie *Frida*. Duncan had chosen Tuesday because it was cheap night at the Paragon, Toonie Tuesdays — full-price for one and a toonie for the other. "I'll get this," said Duncan, flipping open his wallet and sliding out a fifty. Afterwards, they had gone for a coffee at Death By Chocolate, just around the corner. It had gone pretty well.

She'd enjoyed the movie. It wasn't quite Duncan's cup of tea, but whatever, and it did present him with the opportunity to tell Amelia all about Khalo. Prior to that evening he'd never heard of the woman, but in fifteen minutes at the computer he'd learned all he felt he needed to know — enough to impress Amelia. She'd told him she painted a little herself and had a small showing coming up. In fact, it was opening on Friday and would he like to come? *Mmm*, thought Duncan, *cheap wine, cheese, crackers, friends and relatives of the artist. Is that how I want to spend Friday night?* "I'd really love to, but I'm already committed for Friday night." He smiled in as disarming a manner as he could manage, then, realizing the lie required at least some embellishment, added, "A friend from the old school is passing through and we've arranged to have a few drinks. You know, rehash the good old days. Ha. Ha."

"Perhaps another night. It's on for two weeks," said Amelia.

"Oh, of course I'll try and find some time," Duncan replied.

It was on that first date, in the bright light of the eatery, that Duncan had realized that Amelia, with her long coat removed, was a little heavy. He had been thinking about ordering a latte and perhaps a slice of black forest cake, but insisted that Amelia order first.

"Can I get a skim milk latte, please, and I know I shouldn't, but do you have any of that double-chocolate cheesecake?" Amelia asked, grinning coquettishly at Duncan, dimples curving deeply in her round cheeks.

The tall, slim waitress whose perfect, round breasts peeped out from a figure-hugging halter top smiled conspiratorially, "Oh, I think I can find some; that's my all-time favourite as well." She turned to Duncan, leaning forward just a little. "And, sir, what would you like?"

Duncan looked at the waitress and found his gaze darting guiltily from her perfect mouth, to her cleavage, and back, whenever she briefly averted her eyes, which she obliged him by doing from time to time. It was clear, thought Duncan, that a forkful of double-chocolate cheesecake had never crossed her wide, full, glossy lips. He let his gaze rest momentarily on the name badge she wore on her belt, then looked over at Amelia sitting across the table, smiling at him. Latte and chocolate cake were now clearly out of the question. "Oh, just an espresso will be fine, thank you, Katlyn," said Duncan, sitting back, draping one arm across the back of the chair, his right thigh resting over the left, displaying the full measure of his elegant figure. "Never been big on desserts, don't need the calories." He looked across at Amelia in order to relish her small discomfort.

Twenty minutes later, after Duncan had told her a little about his rapid climb to management at the bank, it was time to leave. Leaving the money for the bill on the table, he made a great play of tipping an additional ten percent, which amounted to a dollar-fifty. He winked knowingly at the waitress as she smiled farewell, then prodded Amelia before him out of the door and onto the sidewalk.

"Cheap prick," said the waitress under her breath, before adjusting her neckline down a tad and turning her beautiful smile onto the timid young couple that had just sat down in her corner.

So that had been their first date and now this was the second. Duncan had thought long and hard about going out with a woman who was clearly overweight, but had decided to give it a little longer. By mid-morning, the narrow streets of Granville Island were completely jammed with both tourists and locals driving around and around hoping to spot someone leaving. Duncan stopped abruptly when he saw the brake lights of a parked car flash on, followed moments later by the white reverse lights. He waited irritably, fingers tapping the wheel, as the driver, a bespectacled man, reversed out with agonizing slowness while making frequent small adjustments to his angle of departure. A couple of cars behind him somebody sounded the horn. "Come on, come on, for God's sake," Duncan murmured. Finally, the car moved slowly away and Duncan pulled into the space. "How these people ever get a driving licence is beyond me; they shouldn't be on the road. Anyway, we're here."

Amelia looked at him curiously, "Duncan this is just around the corner ..." but Duncan was already out of the car.

"A dear friend of mine has a little gallery around here. I thought, as it's on the way, we'd stop in ... okay?" said Duncan loudly over the top of the car, "It's in a rather charming little street. You'll love it."

Only feet away from where they'd parked, the couple turned into a small pedestrian-only street. Along one side of the street were a dozen or so small galleries and artisans' studios, and, along the other, the backs of various, older commercial buildings. As they walked, Duncan had been gesturing broadly with his left hand while telling Amelia that he had taken art classes himself for a while. "To be honest, I wasn't all that bad. Probably, if I'd stayed with it ... but you know, you can't do everything ..."

As his relating of his own artistic endeavours dwindled away, so did his expansive gestures. Duncan's hand dangled free for a moment, uncertain what to do with itself, and Amelia seized the moment to shoot out her own hand and take Duncan's. Duncan grimaced reflexively whereas Amelia, in contrast, brightened up. "Duncan, my little showing, well exhibition ... I can't believe of all the places you should take me ..." she started to say happily.

Duncan was intensely agitated that his fingers were trapped in her moist and surprisingly strong grip. He stole a glance at her hand then looking ahead, saw his salvation, "Here we are," he cut in, "Gallery of Light." The gallery was still separated from them by some half-dozen stores, but the fact that it was at least visible, allowed him to forcefully yank his hand free in order to accompany his announcement with a sweeping gesture toward the place. "Did I mention that it is owned by a dear friend of mine?" Duncan repeated as he led the way in through the open doorway.

The gallery occupied a tall room with an all-glass front wall. The interior was taken up with a variety of differently sized, freestanding walls about eight-feet high by four or six-feet wide. These were arranged with no evident attempt at symmetry, and on both sides of their surfaces hung various works of art.

"Robert. Hello, my good friend," said Duncan. "Just passing, thought I'd stop in and say hi."

"Duncan, what a surprise," said Robert Crowley. The speaker was a big man who seemed to wish to emphasize the fact with a wildly patterned, in-your-face shirt that billowed out over his considerable belly. Putting down the stiff bristle brush with which he'd been stabbing at a large dark canvas pinned to the wall, Robert wiped his fingers on a besmeared rag and again on the shirt, which cunningly camouflaged any stain, and walked toward Duncan and Amelia. "And who is your charming companion?"

Amelia rolled her eyes in mock effrontery, as though the question had been a bold compliment.

Ignoring Robert's question, Duncan instead said, "Amelia, this is Robert, a good friend and a very talented artist . . . "

"Well, I don't know about . . . although this year I do seem to have crossed a bit of a threshold . . . financially, that is, thank God." Robert smiled, leaving the impression of becoming modesty.

"He's too modest by far," Duncan said. "I've known him since we were in school together, and it was clear, even then, that he was especially talented. We were quite the radicals back then, eh, Robert?"

Robert didn't reply but smiled briefly.

"As a matter of fact I . . . " started Amelia

"Oh, yes, quite the radicals," continued Duncan. "It wasn't for me, though. As I was saying, Amelia, I recognized that I couldn't be doing everything. I suppose for a while, having some natural talent, I flirted with it, gave art a chance to speak, one might say. I just felt that my future lay elsewhere. I guess I was more into business than art," concluded Duncan a little awkwardly.

Amelia had stepped off to one side and was looking at a large abstract. "I can see that you love to work with light, and you use acrylic. Tell me, Robert, how do you get such vibrancy in your colours? I've tried acrylics and they've never glowed like this."

Robert chuckled, "I suppose you would say, 'tricks of the trade' and not just what I might add to the paint, but it's especially important with acrylics, how you can bring out one colour with another. You must come here one early morning, and I will show you."

"I'd love to," Amelia replied, then moving to another canvas commented, "I love this . . . " she stepped backwards. "You don't give titles to your paintings, I see. There doesn't seem any point really, does there? You've captured the sense of aridity . . . the way everything is sucked dry of all its moisture so perfectly — and the bleakness. It makes me thirsty just to look at it," Amelia giggled. Then looking slightly abashed, she stood silent.

Duncan smiled, "What a charming way to . . . " he began.

Robert cut in, "You're very perceptive, my dear. I painted that in Osoyoos. I think light is everything, of course, and I love the desert. It's a strangely beautiful place. Your friend has a good eye, Duncan."

Duncan looked sideways at Amelia, "Yes, yes, she has."

"Obviously you paint, my dear?" Robert asked.

Amelia blushed. "Well, I do. I mean, I try to paint every day, but I don't, and they're not big pieces, not like yours, of course. Actually, they're rather small. You'd probably think them rather childish, but with this little showing, well exhibition, I'm feeling more ..."

Duncan smiled. The compliment paid to Amelia by his friend, on her insightful observations on his painting, had quite unsettled him for a moment. But now she had exposed herself as a rather inept amateur artist — calling her little showing an exhibition. *My God* — his confidence flooded back. Duncan knew fake, believed he had an unerring nose for it.

"Amelia's a bit of a painter herself, aren't you, sweetheart? Opened a little showing of her own this past weekend. I've been trying to get to it, but, you know, only so many hours in the day," said Duncan.

"Well, actually, Duncan, it's just ..."

"It's really nice of you, Robert, to offer to give Amelia a few tips. I'm sure she'll find that really helpful. I could probably give her a few pointers myself, if I could find the time," Duncan said, smiling tautly.

"I doubt that, but it is true that you have to want to paint. Just like they say writers write, well, painters paint, and nothing is achieved without effort, without complete commitment, discipline," said Robert suddenly severe, and picked up his brush as though he'd reminded himself of the need to resume working.

Duncan was confused. What had Robert meant? That Duncan wouldn't be able to give advice on technique, wasn't competent to offer such advice? Or simply that he, Robert, would not be available?

Amelia broke in on his thoughts, addressing Robert. "Sometimes I regret choosing teaching. But I suppose worry about money and security, you know. Pathetic, isn't it, at my age? I mean I'm not even . . . that's why, in a way, this is a big step for . . ."

"I didn't know you taught," said Duncan

"You didn't ask," replied Amelia.

"Financial security, I mean the need for more than just a necessary degree of it. After all, we have to eat and sleep out of the rain. It's sadly a major force in stultifying so many talents," said Robert. "Perhaps great talent must find a way to express itself, and it will do that regardless of circumstance. But who really knows? Perhaps that is just a statement of belief, rather than anything else. As for lesser talent, it's so easy to be submerged under the imperatives of day-to-day existence."

"Exactly my point," said Duncan, "which of course is why I chose —"

"What do you teach, my dear?" cut in Robert.

" . . . business," completed Duncan.

"Oh, art, of course," answered Amelia.

Looking abruptly at his watch, Duncan announced, "We should be getting along, Amelia. Let's see what this women is like, eh?"

Robert lowered his brush. "Oh, it's lovely, you'll love it. I popped in myself just before closing last night, didn't spend as much time as I'd have liked, quite original subject matter, an almost painful sense of intimacy, and a kind of vulnerability in the composition. In fact, I'll come with you. I'm getting nowhere here. I think I'll have to scrape the whole thing off and start over again." Robert put down the brush he'd just picked up. Amelia looked as though she was about to speak, then thought better of it.

When they arrived at the small gallery adjoining Emily Carr College of Art and Design, it was already obvious that the reviews from Thursday's *Georgia Strait* and the *Globe and Mail* had done their work. There was a diverse crowd of people standing around outside, and a surprising number of people inside the gallery itself. Pinstripe suits, dreadlocks, pyjama bottoms, lots of bare midriffs, pierced belly buttons, and the elusive hints of marijuana were abundantly evident. The president of the college was a cautious man who had never known reckless years, and whose attempt to project an empathy with his student body was limited to his shirt being unbuttoned at the collar. Despite his fixed smile, or perhaps because of it, he was looking singularly ill at ease, as though expecting that at any moment a number of his more outlandish students might be busted by Vancouver's finest. Whether for drugs or for some obscure dress code violations, it would be hard to say.

"Looks as though I wasn't the only one to spot promise," said Duncan smugly. "What do you think, Amelia, have I got a nose for art or not, eh?"

Amelia smiled.

At the desk inside the sliding doors, two older ladies, one with iron-grey hair and one whose hair would have been white had not nature been overruled, sat behind a sign that read Admission by Donation.

Duncan looked pained. "Really, I mean, at what is basically a part of the college, that's a little pretentious ... " he commented loudly.

"All donations go to The Survivors of Incest Society," said the iron-haired lady at the desk. She then added quite sharply,

"It's entirely up to you, sir, how much you wish to donate, if . . . Oh! It's Ms. Pangbourne. My dear, don't wait back there. I missed you tonight. I thought you weren't coming. Come through, come through . . . tsk tsk . . . Excuse me, young man . . . Would you mind a moment? Oh, congratulations, my dear! Such a success, such a success. Congratulations!"

Blushing furiously, Amelia slipped past Duncan and leaning toward the grey-haired lady said, "You're so kind, Ms. Cunningham, thank you, actually these gentlemen are friends of mine. And please call me Amelia."

Knickers

JEFFREY SLAMMED THE DOOR SHUT BEHIND HIM with a force that shook the two frosted-glass panels and left a tingling, prayer-bell echo in the still air. For a couple of moments, he leaned against the closed door, his breath coming in ragged gasps.

"Jeffrey, is that you?"

He could tell she'd been drinking. Not much, maybe, but enough that he could tell. He levered himself off the door and propelled himself toward the foot of the stairs. "Yeah, Mum. I'm going to my room." Jeffrey leapt up the stairs two at a time, his right hand clenched into a fist across his chest.

His mother's voice carried up the stairs after him, "Supper's ready in half an hour."

"I'll be right down. I'm having a shower."

Directly at the top of the narrow stairs was the door to his bedroom. If he'd turned to the right along the small landing, he would have passed the twin doors that opened onto Lillian and Rebecca's rooms, and then his parents' ensuite, to what was usually referred to as the kids' bathroom. Pushing open the door to his room, he barged inside and, closing the door behind him, pressed the lock on the handle. His chest and shoulders still heaving from exertion, and his right hand still making a fist over his heart, Jeffrey threw himself across the bed where he let his fingers open and, in delicate shades of oyster, ivory, and pink, a clutch of women's panties blossomed across his chest.

At almost seventeen years of age, Jeffrey Bannister was the youngest in a family of three children. If anyone had asked, he would have described his childhood in unexceptional terms. Do you love your parents? Of course. Do you love your sisters? Yeah? A typical lanky teenager, Jeffrey resembled his parents in more or less equal measure: his father's hair colouring and straight, pointed nose, but not his strong chin; his mother's fuller lips and pale blue eyes, but not her clean, high cheek bones, which, with the help of only one little visit to her cosmetic surgeon, had stayed with her. Jeffrey was a promising piece of clay, only lightly worked, with a couple of angry pocks and goldsmith's stamps to authenticate his adolescence.

Jeffrey continued to lie there, letting the thumping of his heart return to something like normal while the familiar feelings of panic and excitement abated. As always, he wondered if he'd been seen, recognized by someone he hadn't noticed, and he wondered if tonight or tomorrow there would be a police officer at the door. As he began to relax, his eyes flickered. He crunched up the panties again and held them to his mouth and nostrils, but, disappointingly, he experienced only the unerotic aroma of Tide.

In an office across town, Jeffrey's father, George J. Bannister, rose from his desk. He had the look of a former football player as, indeed, he had been in both high school and college. Once on his feet, the senior Bannister looked at his image in the long mirror on the opposite wall, the one he'd had installed when he took over the office from his predecessor. He had to admit, in his steel-grey tailored suit, he still cut a pretty impressive figure. Even his modest gut, now contained only at the last stop on his black leather belt, seemed to fit his age and stature. Big and sandy-haired, George Bannister managed the local Credit Union. He was satisfied with his life, very satisfied, satisfied to the point that the little affair which he had recently embarked upon, did not even mar his complacency. In fact, to the contrary, he felt it was something he'd earned. A decade younger than himself, his lover's sexual energy seemed boundless, and they made love in ways he could never imagine with his wife, Lynne. George smiled at the memory of their lunchtime tryst a couple of days ago. Parked at one end of a quiet spot overlooking English Bay, she had given him an extraordinarily adept blowjob in the front seat of his Buick. Convenient though fellatio was, it hadn't been easy. Buick's used to be a lot bigger, and he'd suffered a violent leg cramp that had troubled him for a couple of hours afterwards.

Lynne seemed to think that anything other than vaginal intercourse was some kind of goddamn perversion. In fact, sex at all was not something she approached with any degree of enthusiasm. When he could persuade her to take him in her mouth, her response was timid and unexciting, as though she was bobbing for apples.

Perhaps he did feel a little twinge of guilt about his extra-marital fling, but figured that was probably normal. After all, he considered himself a decent man. Besides, Lynne would never know, and, if she never knew, then how was it wrong? Merely thinking about his liaison caused a delightful stirring in his groin. He pulled open the drawer of his desk and reached to the back until his fingers contacted the silky fabric she'd left him as a memento. When he crunched the scrap of fabric over his nostrils, the exotic scent of her sex, mixed with perfume, invaded his senses.

With the sound of the intercom interrupting his reverie, George jerked convulsively and stuffed the panties back in the drawer.

"Yes?"

"Mr. Atkinson's here for his five-thirty appointment, Mr. Bannister. Shall I show him in?"

George looked at the small steel clock on the cabinet behind his desk. A narrow plate attached to the base was engraved with the words, *Best of Luck, George — The Eaton Road Branch, North Park Credit Union.* The ornate hands indicated five twenty-nine.

"Thank you, Shirley. I'll be with him shortly."

"Yes, Mr. Bannister."

Yes, George was satisfied with his life, satisfied with his standing in the community, with what he'd accomplished in his forty-seven years, and with the rewards that went with it. He was satisfied with his neat modern house behind its manicured lawn, with their two current model cars, and, in spite of his little fling, with his attractive wife, Lynne. Her figure wasn't what it had been twenty years and three children ago, but she still looked pretty good. And with that little facelift last year, she could pass for thirty-nine. Well, maybe forty-two. He figured it was money well spent. He could take her anywhere, his brow darkened slightly, as long as he kept an eye on her drinking. George looked at the clock; it was five thirty-four. He thought, again, about the front seat of his Buick. And anyway, enjoying the perks of success was not the same as infidelity.

Turning away from the mirror, George let his gaze take in the room: the tall, glass-fronted bookcase, the credenza, the two leather-bottomed chairs, and the large oak desk behind which he stood. Prominently, on the desk, was a framed photograph of his family — himself, looking very managerial, Lynne, and, of course, his two princesses, Lillian and Rebecca. Lillian was in her second year of university, taking commerce. Little Becky had just finished grade eleven with a B+ average, and was already thinking about which university she'd choose. She was bright, that one — sharp as a tack — who people said took after her dad. George was very proud and very satisfied. He smiled as he looked again at his girls.

Then like a cloud on an otherwise cloudless horizon, a wrinkle appeared on George's forehead. There was Jeffrey, of course, Jeffrey George Bannister, a bit of a fly in the ointment. He was a good kid, but a bit of a worry. Not academically inclined, a dreamer like his mother, with no interest in football or much else that George could see, except that damned noise he listened to, and the earring, for chrissake! He'd occasionally brought home an unattractive, anaemic, androgynous drudge. Some sort of pale gesture toward masculinity, George supposed, although, as the girls in question were usually devoid of any any evident secondary sexual characteristics, and only ever introduced as "a friend", never a girlfriend, even that much was uncertain.

Turning away from the photograph of his wife and girls, he looked again at the small steel clock; the hands indicated five forty-two. That would be about right, he thought.

George Bannister stepped across his office floor and opened the door. A small man in a brown suit rose to his feet. Taking two steps toward him, George stuck out his hand, careful to banish the slight frown that suggested a reluctant preoccupation with more weighty matters, but only once it had been seen.

"Clive, come in, come in. Sorry to have kept you waiting. Please, come right in and forgive the mess. Up to my ears ..."

"Jeffrey! Are you in the shower yet? Your father will be here any minute. Jeffrey! Can you hear me up there?"

Jeffrey was in the middle of a fantasy involving himself and the former owner of the tiny scraps of underwear and wished she'd just shut up! He concentrated again, moving his fist rapidly up and down the shaft of his penis.

"Jeffrey!" his mother called.

Couldn't she leave him alone? It seemed to take forever until he felt the pressure finally release. The blinding, warm tide of relief swept over him. He lay there for several moments, motionless except for the rise and fall of his chest, his left arm flung back over his head, his right fist still crushing a scrap of pewter-coloured fabric over his groin. Then he let out a long exhalation and, with a grunt, pulled himself up off the bed. Yanking open the bottom drawer of his dresser, Jeffrey shoved the soiled panties to the bottom, underneath his socks and underwear, where he kept a couple of well-thumbed pornographic magazines and a handful of his flimsy trophies.

Monday through Thursday, Lynne Bannister generally got home a few minutes earlier than her husband, and on those nights she'd get supper. Friday they'd go out, usually to the Legion, maybe to a restaurant in town, but this was a Tuesday and the ratatouille was simmering in the glass pot. Lynne gave it a couple more turns with the long-handled wooden spoon before replacing the lid and turning off the element. She picked up the glass of red wine and took a sip. Cooking used to be something she enjoyed, but that was before she went back to work. Now it was just a chore, especially after being at the store on her feet all day. She looked at the glass, and with a little shock realized that it was empty again. She picked up the bottle; it was getting down as well. George was bound to say something about that. "Well, screw him," she muttered, pouring herself another glass. She placed the bottle down and took a long sip of the deep red, Australian Cabernet Shiraz.

Lynne didn't share her husband's complacency when she looked at her life, at their life. She didn't mind being the wife of a Credit Union Branch manager. Anyway, she was more than that and, even if she hadn't been to university like George, she could hold her own. She had her own department at the store, and he hadn't given birth to three children. Men had it easy, she thought with sudden bitterness.

But, something had happened, was happening, and she didn't know what. Life had become boring. She used to think of herself as attractive. Now she didn't know. She heard the rush of water in the pipes as her son turned the shower on. She loved the children, but sometimes found herself, hatefully, wishing they were gone, wishing George would just give some time to her, spoil her like he used to, tell her that he loved her, and mean it. She didn't feel cherished. It was all about him. She reached again for the wineglass, but seeing it was almost empty, reached instead for the bottle.

Lynne was the eldest of her parents' two daughters, and had been born and raised in England. Her father had been the manager, well, foreman, in a medium-sized print shop. She remembered her mother washing her father's brown dust coat and hanging it on the line so the neighbours could see that he was management — sort of. She hardly remembered her father, except perhaps his parchment skin, a wispy smile, and a smoker's cough — a grey man in a brown dust coat was mostly what she recalled. She could still see it, pegged to the line, moth brown and bloated, full of summer air. She could see the dust coat more readily than her father; he was like a shadow in her life, pale beside her mother.

When he disappeared from her world, she knew he'd gone, but it wasn't a huge thing. She remembered after he'd died in the big factory-like hospital in the centre of town, her mother coming home with his few personal belongings — all that was left of a life. On an afternoon, not long after the funeral, she found her mother kneeling on the floor of the living room, surrounded by photographs, scraps of paper, and letters. There was a handful of dulled and tarnished campaign medals, their gaudy ribbons greasy and creased, all but untouched for forty years. As well, there was the Military Cross, "for gallantry in action against the enemy" her mother told her. Lynne never knew what the gallant action had been. She still didn't.

When Lynne had sunk down beside her mother, she saw that the older woman was silently weeping, the tears following a convoluted course down her lined face before disappearing into the wool of her cardigan. "This is all that's left of him, all that's left of our life together . . . He was a wonderful man, you know," the old woman paused, then said, "You never really knew him, what he used to be like . . . I'm so sorry." Lynne hadn't understood then what her mother meant, didn't know if she was expressing regret that her daughter hadn't known her father better, or apologizing for somehow failing her or him or both.

The following year her mother died. Her death was the end of a process that had begun with the death of her husband. Lynne felt that her mother had abandoned her. She felt alone — weren't mothers supposed to be there for their daughters? It was different with a man. They were supposed to be ... well ... expendable?

Reminded of the photographs, Lynne placed the wooden spoon on the countertop and, walking a little unsteadily, crossed to the dresser. She pulled open the door where the pictures and other scraps from her parents' life together were stored in an unstable pile of files and biscuit tins. Taking a large round Price's Biscuits tin, she returned to the counter, and, when she removed the tightly jammed lid, a dozen or so pictures burst onto the Formica. They were all there, these frozen fragments of time, fixed in amber squares. Her father, dark-haired and dashing in uniform, with his soldier's brave smile. She could see why her mother might have fallen for him.

Faded and creased was the picture of a sports car with its small crescent-shaped windscreen and leather straps over the hood. Her father was at the wheel, in uniform again, a captain this time, but looking older and more grave. Her mother was all dolled up in a smart suit and Garbo-style hat. She was showing her leg and looking at the camera as she stepped down from the car. Another picture showed her mother on the arm of a tall elegant man with a long narrow nose. "An old boyfriend. He'd have given me anything I wanted. He was minor aristocracy, you know," she had more than once wistfully confided to her daughter. She'd often told Lynne she could have married for money. Had she then married her father for love? It didn't seem likely; she'd never given that impression — not until that day on the living room floor. She'd never seen them kiss.

Lynne shuffled the photographs back into the tin and returned it to the cupboard. Back in the kitchen she took another sip of wine, and was aware of the heat that had come into her face as she did so. The sudden rumble of the garage door opening intruded on her thoughts. "Jeffrey, are you out of the shower yet?" she called, leaning toward the kitchen door.

Brenda Thorpe stared at the space on her washing line where, among other items of her underwear, three pairs of her panties had been drying in the warm afternoon sunlight of an early fall day. There was a perfectly good dryer inside but she liked the softness, and fresh-air scent that the old method of clothes drying gave to clothing. The plastic pegs remained but, tax included, ninety dollar's worth of underwear was gone.

For a few moments, she was completely perplexed. Had she taken them down earlier and forgotten? Was her memory going? She continued for those few moments to stare at the empty space until she finally joined the dots. "Christ!" She whirled around as though expecting to see someone lurking in the shrubbery. "Jesus Christ! I don't bloody believe it!" She tore the remaining clothes from the line and crammed everything into the big yellow washing basket that sat before her on the grass. Then she picked it up, stormed back through the garden into her house, and slammed the sliding door behind her.

The silence of the empty house enveloped her, pressed down around her, and suddenly the only sound was her own breathing and the almost audible thumping of her heart. With a chill, she realised that whoever had taken her panties from the line had come into her back garden, invaded her private space. She slammed the basket down on the kitchen counter, turned on the radio, and cranked up the volume.

The house where Brenda Thorpe had lived for almost seven years — three of these with her then husband and two children, and now with just her younger daughter when she was home from boarding school — was one of a dozen that made up the small cul-de-sac in a long established residential area. Mature trees and shrubbery were a good part of the area's charm and afforded a natural privacy to the extent that Brenda often tanned naked on her patio, confident that only the most determined neighbour would be able to see her. Now the initial anger turned to something more like unease. The dense foliage she had so valued now seemed only to ensure her vulnerability.

Had he looked through her window, smugly sure that no one could see him? Had she left a door or window open? How long ago had he been there? The chill intensified as Brenda remembered that, a month earlier, a pair or two of her panties had seemed to just disappear. She hadn't thought anything of it, assumed that they would turn up. Now she knew with certainty that they wouldn't. Brenda snapped off the radio and listened to the quietness inside the house. For the first time, ever, she felt a little afraid, afraid in her own home.

Still feeling a cold prickling up the back of her neck, Brenda picked up the phone and began to dial 911. She was one digit away from making the connection when she stopped. Was she overreacting? The quietness in the home was now broken by a child's distant laugh, a snatch of birdsong, and the awkward sound of a car starting. She was overreacting. Did she really want the police involved? — "*Can you describe the missing items, Ma'am? Do you have any idea who might want to steal your, er, panties, Ma'am?*" spoken with a snigger hiding behind the policeman's lips, he probably thinking he'd like to fuck her himself given half a chance.

Brenda replaced the receiver. Anyway, she reassured herself, it was bound to be some pathetic jerk who wouldn't know what to do with an actual woman. Some wretched reject who sat on his bed and jerked himself stupid drooling over *Playboy* or whatever boys drooled over these days. Such imaginings restored her confidence somewhat, and she snorted loudly, "You creep," but only the silence of the house answered. Her newly recovered confidence faltered and the prickling up her neck returned. Picking up the receiver again, Brenda dialled a second number.

The phone rang only once before a woman's voice delivered the taped message. "This is the North Park Credit Union. We are now closed for the day. Our office hours are 9:00 AM till 6:00 PM, Monday through . . ."

Brenda slammed the receiver back in its cradle. "Shit!" She looked down at her wristwatch. She stood there for a moment with her eyes closed, then picking up the phone, dialled again.

George Bannister placed the bottle of Conche y Toro Merlot that he had brought in with him on the kitchen counter, and looked at the near-empty bottle of Shiraz and half-empty wineglass standing further along. Christ, it was getting worse. Couldn't she at least make an effort to be sober when he got home? She stirred the ratatouille on the stove with her back to him. *Please God, don't let it be pasta again.*

"Hi, babe," George placed his hand lightly on his wife's hip, noting, without really thinking about it, that the curve that used to be there wasn't anymore.

"Honey, you're home. I didn't hear you come in," Lynne lied, and replacing the lid on the ratatouille, she turned toward her husband and held up her arms to receive his embrace.

George looked into his wife's face, noting the lines, and the high flushed shine that the wine had brought to her skin. He lowered his face to hers and kissed her on the lips. Her lips were wet from the wine and slightly open, but passion was the furthest thing from his mind. The embrace lasted for a couple of moments longer while George patted her head as she rested it on his chest. She smelled like a brewery, a winery anyway, and he hoped her makeup was not transferring itself to his shirt. He thought he should probably say something, but could not get his mind around what to say. What was the point? It wouldn't change anything. He took his hands from his wife's shoulders.

"I see you're a couple of glasses up on me, sweetheart. Perhaps you can pass me a glass."

Lynne turned to the cabinet behind her where the glasses were kept. "Just a glass-and-a-half, honey. You're a bit late today."

George quickly dabbed away the wet from his mouth with the back of his wrist, "It's always the same on a Tuesday, darling, you know that — after we've been closed for two days."

Lynne turned to her husband and handed him the glass.

"Thank you, darling." George poured himself a half-glass, all that was left in the bottle. "To you, darling," he said and waited while his wife put down the paring knife she was holding and raised her own glass to the toast.

Lynne felt a little more at peace now that George was home, and she took only a small sip before returning her attention to the cutting board where vegetables waited to be chopped. "Supper won't be long," she said.

George looked at the curve of the glass in the palm of his hand and his thoughts returned to his lover. They'd met a year ago at a two-day staff conference put on by Head Office. They'd hit it off right away and, for the two nights they were there, George's bed remained unslept in. He knew, of course, she would never replace Lynne and the children, but she'd given him a reward he felt he deserved, that he'd earned. They'd met a number of times since. Conveniently, she lived nearby, even though she worked in the west end. Discretion, of course, was the name of the game.

"So tell me what you're smiling at?" Lynne had half-turned and was looking at him quizzically.

Reluctantly, George brought himself back to the present, "Oh, nothing. Just something that happened at the Branch. Is Jeffrey home?"

At that moment, Jeffrey's tall frame loomed in the doorway. "Hi, Dad." Jeffrey admired his father and would have liked to say more, if only, how was your day? But he didn't. He didn't want to be asked how his day had gone, didn't know how to deal with the fact that he'd been let go after only two weeks on the job. The foreman had told him he wasn't cut out for that kind of work.

"Hey, Jeff, how . . . "

On the countertop next to Jeffrey's elbow, the house phone trilled his reprieve. Jeffrey grabbed for the handset. "Hi?" Jeffrey listened for a couple of moments while Lynne turned once more to the chopping board.

"Yes, he's here," and, holding the phone toward his father, said, "For you, Dad."

Lynne paused almost imperceptibly, raised her head just a fraction, but carried on cutting. George shrugged and took the phone from his son, who seized the opportunity to grab a coke from the fridge and shoot back through the kitchen doorway and up the stairs.

"George Bannister," said George confidently into the mouthpiece.

Had Lynne not kept her attention on the task in hand, she might have noticed the momentary wrinkle of alarm, almost panic, accompanied by a sudden light flush, as soon as her husband heard that instantly recognizable voice.

"Hmm, hmm. Well, I'm sure there's a simple explanation, almost certainly a paper error . . . Hmm, hmm, yes, you're right to be concerned. I'll tell you what, I'll shoot down after supper and look at things myself . . . Hmm, hmm, no, I don't think so. Now don't you worry. I'm completely confident this will be something we can sort out. After I've gone through it, I'll call you . . . Yes, don't worry. We'll get to the bottom of it. Hah, Hah." George recovered himself and was silent for a moment while the other party responded and then, with a final assurance, hung up the phone.

"Who was that?" Lynne asked in as light and as unconcerned a voice as she could muster.

"Oh, it sounds like one of our new tellers has a discrepancy in her day's business," George chuckled. "It's not a little money, so she's understandably upset. I'll sort it out after supper. Poor girl, she'll never sleep tonight if I don't."

"I'd hoped to have a night together," Lynne said, with an edge of irritation keener than she might have allowed, had she not had the best part of a bottle of wine inside her.

"Surely somebody else can go. You don't have to do every-thing yourself." She immediately hated herself for sounding so pathetic but couldn't resist adding, "I thought you were there 'til close?"

Another man might have sensed suspicion but George, his initial alarm forgotten, felt fully master of the situation. "I left a couple of minutes early to pick up the wine before that damn liquor store closed — six o'clock closing. It's ridiculous. Anyway, it will be something she's missed. I don't know. We'll sort it out," George said with growing confidence, as his lie grew into a truth.

"No wonder they think so much of you at the Branch," Lynne said.

"I'm sure it won't take long, an hour or two — tops," said George already thinking of the advantages of a mistress not ten-minutes away, and of what else he'd be doing at Brenda's house aside from worrying about a couple of scraps of underwear.

"Rebecca's staying at Pauline's tonight. And Jeffrey, well, I'm sure he'll be out of the door as soon as he's eaten." Lynne half-turned toward her husband and smiled quickly, awkwardly, with a sort of blurred coquetry, "I thought we might, you know . . . Anyway, I'll wait up for you."

George felt almost overwhelmed with pity. It was not such a long time ago that he could have been excited by his wife, but not anymore. Yet, she was his wife and he felt a kind of pain.

With supper finished and the dishes in the washer, George picked up the keys to the car and glanced at his watch. Lynne was still sitting at the table with her wineglass in front of her. George knew with certainty that she would be passed out within the hour. He rested his hands on her shoulders, "Can I get you a drop more, sweetheart, before I go?"

Lynne smiled awkwardly up at him, her eyes already bleary, "Just a drop. You won't be long, will you, dear?"

George reached for the small rack alongside the window that held a dozen or so bottles. He popped the cork off a bottle of Masi Campofiorin, a wine she couldn't possibly appreciate in her present condition but it assuaged his guilt. He poured his wife a generous glass. "I'll be back before you know it."

Leaving the silver Intrepid at the side of the driveway where, although it could still be seen from the road, it was not obvious. The gravel crunched under his shoes as he walked toward the front door of the house, key in hand. But the door opened before he reached it and he stepped through.

Normally, they would have made love immediately, their passion fuelled by the knowledge of the illicit character of their relationship, and by the necessary awareness of time constraints. However, Brenda was clearly unsettled by what had happened, felt violated and had not made the usual signals that sex was available and welcome.

"I don't think you have to be worried for your safety, sugar, I really don't. From all I've ever heard about these kind of people, they're just inadequate losers. Stealing panties off a clothesline is about as close to a woman as they ever want to be," said George confidently. George seldom felt as good as when he was dispensing advice or comfort. He prided himself on his sensitivity to people and their problems. Which, of course, was why he was here now — she needed his strength. He smiled down at the top of her head, "I'll speak to Tom Barker. He's Chief Inspector over at Marine Drive, and a golfing buddy. Maybe a couple of extra patrols. Frankly,

I don't think we had these problems before that subsidized housing development went in. Hunter's Field. What a damn ridiculous name," pronounced George. "Hunter's Field! You can bet that's where the pathetic creature is from."

She turned her head slightly, and nuzzled into the side of his chest. "I'm so thankful you came, George. I feel so much better. You make me feel so much better."

"I know, sugar, I know," agreed George.

It was Friday, and Jeffrey was alone in the house. His mom was out at some art thing with a couple of her girlfriends. Usually his parents went out together on Friday, but his dad had called and said to go ahead and eat without him — some business thing. Becky, of course, was hardly ever in. It wasn't fair; she was always out with friends and still got a B+ average. Lillian he hardly ever saw, just between semesters. He missed Lillian; she'd always looked out for him when he was little.

Jeffrey pushed the drawer closed. He could feel the familiar pressure in his head, the tightness in his chest. He glanced out of his bedroom window. It was almost dark. He pushed out a long breath through tightly drawn lips, like smokers did, although he didn't smoke.

In the shadow of the trees, Jeffrey knew he couldn't be seen but, at that distance, neither could he see much. He looked at his watch, pressed the button to illuminate the face. Eight forty-five, and, even this late in the evening, the weather was still mild. He wore blue jeans, a dark-green sweater, and a grey baseball cap — the same clothes he wore every time.

She was in. He'd seen her a couple of times already, on her own as usual. He'd seen a girl there once, her daughter he guessed, maybe a couple of years younger than him and what a knockout, like her mother. He saw the flickering of a television screen, the phantasm it suggested on the opposite wall. Looking around once more, he trotted quickly across the lawn until he was up against the side of the house, his heart pounding in his chest. Inching forward, Jeffrey peered around the door frame. The woman was in the kitchen preparing a meal. Jeffrey watched the movement of her arms and shoulders as she lifted handfuls of brightly-coloured vegetables off a thin marble slab and dropped them into a wok. She was wearing tight cotton jeans and a white blouse. He held his breath as she reached up into a cupboard, and watched the way the material of her blouse stretched over her breast, and how the muscles of her buttocks tightened under her jeans. He felt the beginnings of sexual excitement and briefly let his hand slide down to touch himself.

Leaning a little further forward, he gripped the frame of the sliding door to steady himself. It moved a fraction before knocking against the lock. The woman turned quickly at the sound, before he could even think. She didn't scream but put her hand to her mouth and looked straight at him.

For a fragment of time, Jeffrey stood transfixed. In that same fragment, the woman snapped on a light switch. The deck lights blazed on with all the ferocity of an explosion. Shocked and horrified, Jeffrey crashed backwards, tripped over a planter, and tumbled over the low deck rail onto the grass. His left wrist buckled under the full weight of his body and he heard it snap as he hit the ground.

Stunned and disoriented, he lay there, vaguely aware that his left wrist didn't feel right, and tried to make sense of what had happened. He was only half aware of low rumbling as the sliding door opened.

Brenda Thorpe looked down at the boy. He didn't look old enough to shave. Something about him was vaguely familiar; he must be from the neighbourhood. Although the blood was still drumming in her ears, she was relieved to see that she no longer had reason for fear. In any event, he appeared to be in something like shock.

As the boy gathered his wits, his confusion gave way to panic, and it was clear he was about to run. He was holding his left wrist awkwardly, and fell over again as he began to stumble to his feet. Amazingly, she felt sorry for him. She guessed he was about the same age as her daughter.

"There's no point in running, I know where you live," she lied. She took a step forward, amazed at how calm she was, how much the master of the situation she felt. She noticed the strange angle of his left hand, "Can you move your fingers?"

The boy gaped at her stupidly, uncomprehending.

"Can you move your fingers?" Brenda repeated.

The boy looked at his hand.

"I think you might have broken your wrist. You're going to have to go to the hospital with that. You may as well come and sit down."

Muddied and grass-stained, the boy slowly got to his feet and stepped onto the deck. He then sat in one of the plastic patio chairs Brenda had pulled aside, his left arm cradled in his lap.

"So, what were you doing out here?" Brenda asked.

The boy didn't answer.

"A Peeping Tom, are you?" and then suddenly realizing, Brenda asked dryly, "Are you the one who's been collecting my underwear?"

The boy stared down at the floor.

"Well, are you?"

The boy continued to stare at the floor.

"It is you, isn't it?" she repeated.

Still staring at the floor, the boy nodded.

Brenda stood there, letting this sink in. She shook her head slowly from side to side. "Stay there," Brenda commanded, before stepping back through the sliding door into the kitchen and opening the fridge. Coming back outside, she handed him a tall glass of orange juice. "Why?" she said, holding onto the glass even as the boy closed his hand around it and his fingertips touched hers.

The boy, in his misery, didn't speak.

Brenda released her hold on the glass and the boy slurped half the juice down, some dribbling down his chin.

Now that she knew with certainty that she had control, she was no longer afraid. However, she was growing irritated at his continued dumbness. Folding her arms across her breasts, she leaned against the frame of the sliding door. *Thank God she had daughters,* she thought.

"Why?" she repeated.

"I don't know," the boy said suddenly in a strangulated voice. Then added, "I like you."

"Pah! You like me? So because you like me you steal my underwear so you can ... what ... jerk off?"

The boy looked up, his features twisted in pain and humiliation, "I ... I don't ... please don't, I ..." Then he went quiet. When he spoke again, it was with the flatness of defeat. "Are you going to call the police?"

"What do you think?" Brenda spoke with barely contained ferocity. "You know you have a problem, don't you? I mean, you know it's not normal to go around stealing women's underwear, don't you ... whatever your name is? What is your name? And don't lie to me," she commanded abruptly.

"Jeffrey," the boy answered, too dazed, too dominated to even think of lying. He looked away from the glare of the deck lights, his face hidden in shadow.

Again, Brenda knew that she had seen him before. *Screwed-up kid,* she thought. Yet something was eerily familiar about him. Quietly, she watched him for a moment and, in the brief silence, she heard the gravel crunching on her driveway at the front of her house. She didn't need to go to the door; he had a key. She was glad he was here. He'd know what to do.

. "Jeffrey, my friend's here. I think the first thing we have to do is get you to Emergency and get your wrist looked at. We can see about the police at the hospital." She heard the front door close. "I'm through here, honey," she called out.

At that moment, a shadow loomed in the doorway behind her. The familiar strong male voice, "Hi, baby . . . What? What's this? What's going on?"

Thank goodness, thought Brenda, as she turned around looking up into his face. "George, your timing is perfect. This young man is . . . "

A Wee Bit of Fun

"HEY, MICK, DOLBY, SHUT UP. If they think there's three of us, they'll fuck right off," Vince hissed.

I have to admit it, Vince was the man, the one who'd come up with the idea. So we stayed put, and anyway, we had the bottle of rum, a bronze promise in the dark. I sat on a blunt remnant of ancient elm, and Dolby was across from me in a small, triangular clearing, leaning against this big rock that was smooth and round like a half-formed Buddha. With the last daylight gone, a veil of pale moonlight leaked through the branches and it felt as if we were in a ruined chapel with a burned-out roof, preparing for some satanic rite, which as it turned out, was not so far off the truth. Me and Dolby were in shadow, but ten yards away where Vince stood, the pathway was illuminated, bathed in white light — and so was Vince.

Our evening had started a couple of hours earlier, after Vince had picked us up in his truck. We were going to start the evening with a couple of drinks at the Palace, at the corner of 4th and Cypress. We usually went out for a drink on a Friday, to celebrate the end of the workweek, the forty-hour grind. I'm telling you, if I never have to sell another La-Z-Boy or end table, it'll be too soon. It was one of those

Vancouver evenings that makes you glad to be living here and not in some commuter hell out in Maple Ridge or Coquitlam. Driving along Beach and looking out across English Bay, I could see a tug towing an enormous log boom. You couldn't tell that they were even moving. Could you imagine driving one of those things as a job? Five miles an hour up and down the Strait, I mean, I'd go completely bananas.

Further back, miles behind the tug and its tow, under the bronzed light of the western sky, the Gulf Islands were a low dusty stencil. Yeah, no question, it was one of those great summer evenings, the glass high-rises on fire with the pink and gold of the dying day. Magic really.

There wasn't much magic about the Palace, though. The Palace was a bar in the old style and I don't mean that as a compliment. A shoebox of a building thrown up in the sixties with nothing much done to it since. The made-in-India carpet was deep red with a black and beige pattern, raw in a couple of places, and dull with the patina of age — ground-in dirt, cigarette ash, and beer slops. The walls and ceiling looked like the inside of a smoker's lung. Myself, I don't smoke; I think it's a loser's habit. The Palace was a popular bar, though, especially with students. Of course, that was more to do with the beer being a dollar less than anywhere else, which was why we were there. The waitress put three more beers in front of us. Vince had got the first round, so this one was mine.

"That'll be eleven twenty-five," announced the little blonde, all smiley.

I figured she was probably a student herself, maybe nineteen or twenty and a seven on a scale of ten. Maybe a six-and-a-half — I can be a bit picky. I pulled out my wallet and peeled off a twenty. "Give me five back," I said. She gave me a real nice smile and, leaning forward while she reached in the little pouch where she kept her money, she let me see a little more of her tits. *Very nice*, I thought, then watched her little bottom as she walked away.

"What a bunch of dykes," said Vince, his voice a blade gutting my little reverie. "Fucking students. The guys look like girls and the girls look like they'd be happier fucking each other than getting fucked by this bunch of faggots. Fuck! Talk about no fucking talent."

That was typical of Vince. He's a different kind of cat and he can be a mean fucker. He'd have something negative to say about any place or any situation. To tell the truth, the talent wasn't bad, but I didn't say anything.

Vince took a swallow of beer and made a face. "And this beer tastes like piss."

"Fucking place. We should head down to the Well. There's some hot little chicks down there," said Dolby.

That was Keith Dolby talking. Now understand this about Dolby: whether or not the girls were hotter at the Palace or the Well was really beside the point. The point was that Dolby wouldn't be chatting them up. When he gets to talking about girls, he's full of shit. The way he drinks, he always gets pissed before he even gets close to getting any. Dolby and I have known each other since grade eight, and I can honestly say that, even though we're the same age, I don't think he's ever actually got laid. Can you believe that? I think Dolby might only ever have dated his fist. It's not that there's anything seriously wrong with him, like he's not a bad looking dude and all that, but what girl wants a drunk all over her? Hey, but that's Dolby. As Vince said, "You don't really choose your mates do you? They just happen."

Dolby's mother and my mother used to be friends, still are, I suppose, although not as tight as they used to be. Our parents got divorced about the same time. Divorce. Such a nice French-sounding word, to cover all the screaming and blaming and grasping and thieving that it really is, and all that crap about putting the children's interests first. Yeah, right. Believe that and I've got a nice piece of swampland for you. After their divorces, my mom and Dolby's mom used to go out together looking to get laid. In those days, they had those big Farah Fawcett hairstyles that they thought made them look hot. Hot? They looked just plain ridiculous.

Dolby and me left school together a few years back, at sixteen. We went different ways with jobs and stuff but we still hung out together. But this night, the one I'm telling you about, Dolby, the idiot, had just signed up with the Canadian Armed Forces. I'd told him he must be soft in the head. Anyway, he had exactly five days of civilian life left and was determined to party his head off up to the last minute. That was all right with me. Like I said, he was my bud, he deserved a good send off. But he was still an idiot.

I've known Dolby just about forever. I remember his dad, although where he is now beats me and I don't think even Dolby knows. At least I still see my old man the odd time. Dolby's new family really isn't so new anymore, either. It's been about three years, maybe four. His new family is what has become fashionably known as blended. In Dolby's case, that involves him, his mom — minus the big electro-cuted hairdo — and two hot stepsisters, just into their teens, their dad, associated visiting exes, grandparents, in-laws and — wait for it — twenty-nine animals. Dolby's stepsisters have a thing for animals, or maybe it was just a way of driving Dolby out, because I know for a fact he can't stand all those fucking budgies. And the cats? There are four of them — even one makes his eyes water and plugs up his sinuses. I've been at his house and tried to carry on a conversation in the kitchen where they keep the budgies. I didn't know this, but the more budgies hear you natter the more they natter. And if that wasn't enough, they also have a bunch of chickens pumping out eggs in a coop in the garden. Every time I go there, all these chickens rush over in a group and stare at me, making little clucking sounds. It's kind of spooky, like a farmyard version of that old movie by Hitchcock, you know, *The Birds*. Well this version's *The Hens* and it's spookier. Dolby's stepsisters know eleven different ways that eggs can be served for breakfast. "Don't peck at your food" is an expression that takes on a whole new meaning in Dolby's life.

That's not the end of it either, there's tropical fish and a retriever-something cross that's as broad as it's long. Then there's hamsters which make the place smell rank so it's hard to breathe, a pet rat, and as both of the girls ride, somewhere down the road probably a horse, probably two — but why stop there, why not a herd? I think the reason they're called blended families, is because it involves throwing everything and everybody into a blender turning it up to high and seeing what kind of fucked-up human beings come out the other end. Well, we know what comes out the other end — a Dolby, he's an example, twenty-years of age and still a virgin shaking hands with his dick every night.

I think climbing out of the blender and into the army must have seemed like a way out for Dolby. Mind you, I'm the first to admit, you can't stay at home forever. And I knew that Dolby's step-dad would be happy to see him go. I could see why; guys shouldn't be living at home at his age, not with those two hot little stepsisters that Dolby probably fantasizes about when he's polishing his carrot. His stepdad may be an asshole, but that doesn't change the truth.

Myself? I left home at sixteen, right after I left school, and that seemed late enough. I wasn't going to stay with my mom while she ran around like a silly tart. My dad was hardly out of the door when she had her first big-hair fan banging her in the bed she'd shared with dad for as long as I could remember. I mean how crass is that? That fuckwit lasted two months. She didn't hang around either, I don't know if she even had time to change the sheets before she had the next guy in there giving it to her. He was an even bigger idiot than the first — at least the first one knew I hated his guts. The second jerk couldn't figure that much out. He sat down and said we should have a man-to-man, the moron. And my mom later, all smiles, asking how it went with Geoffrey? I mean how did she think it went? What the fuck did she think it was — musical fucking dads? Fuck!

Not that my old man was all sweetness and light. For a guy who made his living writing, he wasn't exactly a bedtime story kind of guy. In fact, he could be an asshole, but she married him and she should have stayed with him; he was my dad, our dad — Cindy and me. Most of the time he wasn't an asshole, just some of the time. I don't know anyone who isn't an asshole some of the time. I mean, who's perfect? Anyway, bottom line, I couldn't handle living in the same house with that idiot Geoffrey. Cindy didn't much like it either, but she was twelve. What could she do?

When I left school, Dad got me my first job as a gofer at the *Vancouver Star* pressroom, which was where he was a sports reporter. Christ, he just about bloody lived there. How he kept his job, I don't know. After the divorce, he was pissed more often than he was sober. Before the divorce, he'd come home a little worse for wear maybe once or twice a month. Afterwards? I hardly ever saw him when he hadn't been drinking. When I'd started working at the paper, I thought I could have moved in with him, but he made it pretty clear that wasn't on. He said he was glad he'd been able to help with the job an' all, but that I was on my own as far as he was concerned. He'd moved onto his boat and pulled up the gangplank, just enough room for him, his bottle of vodka, and his typewriter.

"Son, work it out for yourself — life's a bitch and then you die."

What a novel observation. Great help. Thanks Dad.

"What?" he said, reading my thoughts, "You prefer I sugar coat it?"

Anyway I didn't stay at the job. It was going to be ages before I made any money and being a reporter didn't seem like a great goal. Where did it get my dad? That's when I went to The Brick.

"So what do you say? How about I get another round in, then we head down to The Well?" concluded Dolby, his face flushed and shiny with alcohol, his voice distorted by it, his arm waving around to catch the girl's eye.

"I'm okay with that," I said, although honestly, I was quite content to stay at the Palace. "It's 10:00 now, it'll just be starting to fill up. What do you say, Vince?" I hated the way I always deferred to Vince but that's the way it was — we both deferred. I don't think it bothered Dolby. It bothered me, though.

I've known Vince for almost as long as I've known Dolby. He came to the school in eighth grade. He'd come with his father from back east. Third generation Canadian but you wouldn't know it. Despite his English last name, which is Taylor, his origins are Scottish. I mean, he's Canadian through and through, but his grandfather had been born in Scotland and you got the feeling that Vince wished he had been too. Vince is short and muscular with bright red hair to kind of watermark his heritage. He got a job in construction as soon as he left school and that's what he's done since. More money than Dolby and I put together and he still lives at home with his dad, which helps 'cause I don't think he has to pay anything. His dad doesn't say much, but you get the feeling that the apple didn't fall far from the tree and that Vince is probably just like his old man was when he was our age. Vince's mother died of cancer when he was eleven. Funny, really, the two of us who have mothers, we're embarrassed by them, but Vince he doesn't have one and wishes he did. That's life, eh, it's like my dad said: it's a bitch. Vince always has money and he's the only one of us with a vehicle, a twelve-year-old Dodge pickup. I wouldn't want to work in construction my whole life, but in the good weather it's probably okay and it pays all right.

"What do you say we have a bit of fun first lads, the lasses aren't going anywhere, not 'til a lot later," said Vince, leaning forward, nursing his sleeve of pale ale between both hands.

Vince drinks less than either Dolby or me. In fact, he seldom has more than one or two beers over the same time that Dolby and me have easily got through four or five.

"Hey, I'm all for fun," said Dolby.

"What kind of fun Vince . . . what do you have in mind?" I asked, cautiously, because I knew Vince — his idea of fun might involve more than I, or even Dolby, were ready to commit to.

"Well," said Vince slowly, "I was thinking we might have a wee bit of fun with the faggots running around the bushes in Stanley Park, trying to get their ends away."

Even though Canadian through and through and without the least trace of a Scottish accent most of the time, Vince loaded his speech with words and expressions, calling up his heritage. "And I was thinking that a wee word from the guardians of public morality — that's us — might just ruin their fucking night, eh?" Vince concluded, smiling, thinly.

Dolby lifted his glass of ale, "Fucking right on! What those queer fuckers get away with is fucking disgusting. It's like there's one law for them and another for us. Could you imagine getting away with banging a chick out in public? The cops'd be on you like flies on shit," said Dolby loudly before slamming his fifth glass back onto the table and wiping away the rim of froth from above his top lip.

Dolby, you're an idiot, I thought.

"That's my point, mate, you've got all those fucking idiots in Victoria and Ottawa or wherever the fuck making the rules and they're all queer as three-dollar notes themselves. Anyway, the faggots need a little reality adjustment. Fuck, if it goes on like this, you'll need to be a fudge packer to get a job," said Vince, still nursing his glass.

I'd been keeping pace with Dolby more or less, but now he was sitting with his fifth beer glass empty on the table front of him and I was stuck halfway through my fourth. The fifth beer, which Dolby had ordered for me stood untouched, like a spare prick at a wedding. However, even though he was somewhat pissed, which he was every time we went for a drink, Dolby was alert enough to inquire again just what Vince's bit of fun entailed. "So, Vince, what do you have in mind, exactly?"

"Hey, nothing heavy, man. Just find one of the fuckers and tell him we're vice, undercover or whatever, you know, make him turn his pockets out, tell him we've got to search him. Fuck, I don't know, throw his clothes in the lagoon or something. Hey, maybe throw him in after them," Vince laughed. So did Dolby, and I guess maybe I did too.

"Fucking right! Fucking faggots," said Dolby, getting all excited so that a couple of guys at nearby tables looked over in our direction. Vince just looked back real hard and they looked away.

"I don't know, man," I said. I didn't really have anything against faggots; they just played for a different team was all. And I was kind of surprised at Dolby, even if he was pissed. I think maybe he was really nervous about joining the army and this was his way of covering up.

"Hey, I'm only joking, Mick, you idiot, I'm just meaning fuck with them a bit, that's all — just a wee bit of fun, mate." Vince took a small sip of beer. "Fuck, Mick, we might not even find one of the fuckers," he added, smiling. "Better yet, fuck the faggots, let's pick up a forty-pounder. I've got some weed in the truck; we'll have us a little private party down on the beach, that way it doesn't matter if we find a faggot or not. We'll just give this poor bastard," Vince nodded at Dolby, "a send-off before he heads over to Bosnia to get his nuts vaporized."

· I chuckled at that and Dolby kind of snorted.

"You think I'm joking, mate?" said Vince, looking at Dolby, "What do you think happens in one of those troop carriers when a fucking great bomb goes off underneath it? Everything below your waist is gone, man. I mean it. You'll come back looking like a fucking fire hydrant, and with even less chance of ever getting laid, ever! It'll be game over for that, mate — Specialist, Peckerless, first class. Anyway, I told you not to join. You could have come and worked with me and now you're going leave your nuts fertilizing a fucking farmer's field in Bosnia, man," said Vince smiling thinly, then adding, "Not that you're fertilizing fuck all else Dolby."

"Yeah, fuck off, Vince," said Dolby, all pissed-off looking.

"Here, Dolby, show me your hand," said Vince.

Compliantly, Dolby held out his right hand, which Vince cursorily examined.

"No, there's nothing growing there, mate," said Vince all serious.

I laughed as Dolby snatched back his hand.

"Just don't say your old mate Vince didn't warn you, you fucking idiot."

"Anyway," said Dolby, keen to turn the conversation away from his sexual habits, but spoken with a graze of uncertainty in his voice, "what the fuck do you know about troop carriers? They're solid steel, man, like fucking tanks."

I felt kind of sorry for Dolby. If it hadn't been for his fucked-up family, he wouldn't be joining the army, no way. "I can't believe you're going, Dolby," I said. "Don't listen to Vince; he's just giving you a hard time. Those trucks are state of the art, man. And, anyway, that peace-keeping shit will be over before you finish basic training."

"Hey, what the fuck. I'm just going to serve my country," said Dolby.

"Serve my country? Oh, fuck right off, Dolby, what the fuck have you been smoking?" said Vince. Then rising from his seat he added, "Hey, what you can do for your fucking country is pitch in for the rum. I'll pick it up." Dolby and I pulled out our wallets and handed over a twenty each. "See you in two minutes at the truck." And with that Vince exited to the liquor store next door.

We left the truck facing the lagoon, just inside the park, and walked the rest of the way in. With me and Dolby both feeling pretty good and giggling stupidly, we wound up at where I said at the beginning — this little triangular spot in the bush beside the trail that ran along Lost Lagoon. That was when Vince told us to stay in the bushes and shut the fuck up.

With Dolby still giggling, that's what we did. Vince stayed out on the trail, loitering with clear intent, looking like a male prostitute. I felt a bit embarrassed for him to tell you the truth. I mean, I know Vince isn't gay but he looked it. He lit up a small joint and the familiar sweet smell carried easily back to us on the slight breeze. Vince had left his vest in the truck and stood in jeans and a white T-shirt stretched across a torso developed and hardened by three years of construction and three-times-weekly workouts at the gym.

"Hey, Vince, give us a toke," Dolby called out in an exaggerated stage whisper. He was so fucking drunk it was pathetic.

"Shut the fuck up," Vince hissed for the second time. "Someone's coming."

We fell silent, well almost — except for snickering at fag jokes.

"Hey, Mike, did you hear the one about the young guy who wanted a life of adventure? So he signed on with this ship that was going off for a six-month cruise and there were no women . . . "

"Fuck, Dolby, you told me that one at the Palace. Pass the rum, you dumb fuck," I whispered. The bottle of Lamb's that we passed back and forth clinked on the stones but the dude walking down the trail toward us didn't seem to notice.

He was taller than Vince, but slighter. He was dressed like he was out for a run, in shorts and singlet and running shoes, but obviously looking for something else because he wasn't running. I watched as he came close. I thought he was about to pass when he looked across at Vince. I could see that Vince looked back just long enough to make a connection.

"Hey," said Vince, holding out the joint, "you want a toke?"

I could see the glint of the guy's smile in the dark, and then he walked toward Vince. He took the offered joint and inhaled briefly, holding the smoke in his lungs for a moment or two before letting it unfold into the evening air. "Thanks, friend. The name's Russell." His voice was all thin and kind of reedy.

"Hi Russell, it's Vince," said Vince. "I guess we're both here for the same thing, eh?"

"I think we can safely assume that, Vince, don't you think?" said Russell and reaching out, placed his hand against Vince's crotch.

I thought Vince would pop him one right then. But he didn't.

"I think you've got something here that needs taking care of," said Russell.

Dolby near wet himself when he came out with that, and we could see Russell's hand moving up and down the front of Vince's jeans. Dolby was almost doubled up with one hand over his mouth the other holding his stomach trying hard to suppress his laughter. He was pretty hammered.

I felt kind of bad for the guy, and I didn't find it that funny, not like Dolby did. I mean, not hysterical.

"Aye," said Vince, "we'll see, eh. Let's get off the trail; I've got a wee spot just back here, out of sight."

"So are you Scottish, Vince?" asked Russell.

"Yeah, whatever," said Vince. I could hear that familiar, muted strain of anger in Vince's voice, and wondered why the guy didn't hear it too. Why he didn't get the fuck out of there.

Now Dolby and I didn't make a sound but, even so, I was surprised the dude didn't somehow sense our being there — we were only feet away. I guess he was preoccupied, on his knees in front of Vince, his fingers busy undoing the buckle of Vince's thick leather belt. That's when Vince said, "Heads up you fucking faggot — it's show time." Vince's locked his hand in the faggot's hair and jerked his head savagely backwards.

Then Dolby stumbled to his feet and burst out into the clearing and I scrambled out after him, but I hardly knew why. What was *I* going to do? The guy must have just about wet himself. It was pretty clear we weren't there to help him, not with Dolby grinning like an idiot, and a bottle of booze dangling by his side.

"We're vice, you queer asshole, and we're here to straighten you fucks out," said Dolby his voice pitched uncharacteristically high, the tendrils of hysteria woven through his words. He took a slug from the bottle of Lamb's.

"You're not vice, you're not even cops," the dude said tightly.

"You calling my friend a fucking liar, faggot?" Vince said, pulling the guy's head farther back at the same time.

Now, there's no question I was more than a little worse off for the booze. I'm not a big drinker, really, and hard liquor is not something I do well with, but I could see this was going to turn into something really nasty. "Hey come on, guys, the fucker's shitting himself. Let's go party," I said, "Let's get the fuck out of here."

"Mick, you're not listening, man," said Vince, smiling broadly — and I've noticed that before, with Vince the meaner he gets, the more he smiles. "This piece of faggot shit just called Dolby a liar, says we're not vice. Now how would he know that, man, I ask you? He must think he's a real clever dick, eh? I think a little attitude adjustment is definitely well in order here, wouldn't you say?"

"I'm sorry, I didn't mean that you . . ." started Russell, but got no further. Vince brought his knee back and slammed it hard into the guy's exposed and vulnerable chest — I swear I heard his ribs crack — before throwing him to the ground where he lay moaning and gasping for air.

"Oh shit, man," I said, "Come on, Vince, let's leave it, man. He's learned his lesson." Now, I've gotta admit, no fucking question, I was scared. I wanted to be anywhere else but where I was.

But Vince said, "That was just a love tap, Mick. We haven't started having fun yet."

Dolby belched and took another swig of rum. "Man, Vince is right, man. He called me a fucking liar, I'm going to get my nuts blown off upholding fucking democracy and defending dickheads like this, and him call me a liar? Well, piss on that," said Dolby, who then walked over to where Russell lay curled in a foetal position, his hands crossed over his chest, sucking and gasping for breath. "Piss on that," repeated Dolby, staggering and pulling down the zipper of his pants, "Call me a fucking liar, you fucking prick," he mumbled as he let go a stream of urine across Russell's crumpled body, a veil of vapour lifting up into the moonlight.

Vince burst out laughing, "Oh, right on, Dolby, fucking right on."

Dolby, grinning stupidly looked across at Vince. "Piss on that, eh Vince," he said pulling up the zipper of his fly.

"Oh shit, man," I said again thinking I'd never seen Dolby like this, even with the booze; this wasn't a Dolby I knew.

"The problem with these fuckers is that they fuck children, that's why I've got no time for the perverts. You fuck little kids don't you, asshole?" Vince leaned down over the moaning figure of Russell Carmichael. "Man, you smell bad, you know that? You smell like piss, you know that?"

"Yeah, the fuckers should have their fucking dicks cut off, that would solve a lot of problems," screamed Dolby excitedly, sucking back more rum and pushing Vince to one side. "Hey, try this, asshole," and the kick landed with crushing force in Russell's groin. "Ha, ha. Did you like that? Here, try another. Ha, ha, ha, here's one more."

Now Dolby was laughing hysterically, Russell was screaming and Vince was moving quickly, clamping his hand over the man's mouth. "Shut the fuck up, faggot," Vince rasped in his ear, and then turning back toward me, "Come on, Mick, get in the party mood, man."

I didn't know what was happening, I swear to God I didn't know what was happening, or why. It was a nightmare, this wasn't meant to happen, everything was wrong, had gone wrong. I heard myself speak, but you know I was hardly aware that it was me speaking, it could have been someone else, I didn't even recognize myself, my voice was all high like a girl's. "Vince, this is no party. I'm not into this, man. This isn't right, man. This just isn't right, Vince." Then I remember stepping backwards, then stumbling, and the next thing I knew I was sitting on the grass. That's when I knew I was drunk. I knew I shouldn't have been sitting on the grass.

"Mick, you are such a fucking wuss," said Vince.

Then it seemed like Dolby came to his senses a bit, a kind of belated awareness that maybe things had got way out of hand. "I don't know Vince," Dolby said, sounding suddenly sober. "This dude's making an awful noise man."

"Yeah, he needs a fucking dip to bring him out of it That'll sort him right out. Here, Dolby, give me a hand."

I watched the two of them pull the guy, who looked only barely conscious, out of the bush and across the trail to the edge of the Lagoon. I got to my feet but I wasn't really steady, and I crashed into some bushes and fell again, and scratched myself all to shit — my face and everything. I called out to Vince, "What are you going to do, Vince? You're not going to throw him in are you?"

"You're not, are you, Vince?" I heard Dolby ask plaintively.

"Don't be a fucking idiot, Dolby, and it's not *me*, it's *we* that are going to duck the fucker."

"You mean we're just going to duck him and that's it, right?" said Dolby

"Yeah, that's right Dolby. Now just help me shovel the fucker in," said Vince.

"Hey, he's awake, man, he's okay. He's awake," Dolby cried out.

I didn't know what to do. I mean I didn't want any part of this shit but I couldn't just walk away could I? You can't just bail on your friends, can you? Not when it's something you started together. You can't, can you? I followed across the trail to the lagoon. I heard the dude start to speak, "What are you doing, please, what's happening . . . ? Oh no, please no." I was still feeling like shit but I'd been scared sober. I could hear Dolby whining.

"I don't know, Vince, I don't know. It wasn't meant to be like this, it was meant to be a bit of fun," said Dolby hopelessly.

"Wake up, Dolby. Have you seen what you did to his fucking nuts?" snapped Vince harshly. "That doesn't look like fun to me, man. I can't see the fucking judge cracking up over that, eh. What the fuck do you think?"

I watched Dolby look down at the dude. Even though Dolby was nearer, I bet in the darkness he couldn't see much more than I could, but that was enough. He suddenly said, "I feel sick man," and then he walked away a couple of paces and threw up. I smelt the rank smell of rum and vomit waft over to me. The next thing I knew, Dolby started to back away, then he turned and went blundering back along the trail toward Georgia Street. Vince called out to him, but he didn't look back.

Vince looked across at me. "Call yourself friends, eh? Let me do all the heavy lifting? Fuck! So what kind of fearless warrior is old Dolby going to make when he starts throwing up at a spot of blood. Answer me that, eh?" said Vince. He looked down at Russell who was moaning lightly, laying on his back, his upper body half-in and half-out of the water, eyes open looking at him.

"What are you going to do, Vince?" I asked, real soft.

"Well, what do you think I should do, Mick, leave my driving licence with him and go call the police?"

"Please don't do it, don't hurt me anymore," the dude whispered.

"You're in this too, Mick, as well as our fearless friend."

"Ah, please don't do it, please don't," the dude croaked.

Vince looked down at him, then sank to his knees in the wet marsh grass, next to the guy. I watched Vince reach forward, clasp the guy's head between his hands, and pull him upwards a little out of the water. For a moment or two, I thought Vince was helping him, pulling him out, then he leaned forward and kissed him hard on the mouth before letting his head fall back into the sodden grass.

Jesus, that was weird. I felt my head spin. "Vince, what . . . " I started to say and then clamped my mouth shut.

Vince levered himself upright, wiped his mouth with the back of his hand, and after a brief contemplative pause, carefully placed his foot on the dude's face, pushing his head through the reeds and under the water. My guts went cold and my whole body started shaking, but I stayed rooted to the spot. "Aw, fuck, Vince . . . " I saw the dude grab at Vince's foot, but Vince braced himself with his other foot and pressed down harder until the thrashing ebbed, and finally stopped altogether.

"Fucking faggot," said Vince, then pulled out his cigarettes and lit one up.

I turned and ran. The lights of Georgia Street and the traffic heading for the bridge swam before me and every-thing was a blurred kaleidoscope of colour. At one point, I stumbled into the gutter and fell down hard. I crawled a couple of paces then sat on the curb, right there on Georgia trying to pick the bits of stone from my kneecaps and the heels of my hands. It hurt like shit and suddenly I realized I was crying and blubbering.

"You all right, man?" a voice asked.

I looked up at this guy and his girlfriend who were standing and looking at me from the sidewalk.

"Yeah, thanks, yeah, I'm all right."

"You sure? You don't look so good, you're all cut up. Do you want us to get you home?"

"No, no thanks, I'll be all right."

Then the guy reached down and put his hand on my shoulder. "Are you sure, guy? You look a bit of a mess. You shouldn't be out here in the state you're in; someone's going to do you a mischief."

The Well

"WELL, THAT'S IT THEN," SAID RUFUS as he placed the document down on the small vinyl covered table that separated them. "I guess I'm now the owner of a little bit of France."

"*Oui, mon ami*, that is the truth," the small dark-haired man across the table replied, reaching forward to pick up one of the two small glasses that stood on the table before them. "A toast to your purchase, and may you and Jennifer, enjoy your life here in Cipières."

Rufus lifted his glass, acknowledged the toast with a small sip of the dark, bronze brandy and then added, "And to you, my friend, for all your work in making this possible. I hope your other clients bring you less problems."

Jean-Paul moved his shoulders fractionally, accompanying the gesture with a small self-deprecating smile, and took a second sip before replacing the glass on the table. "My friend, I would not have wished it to be otherwise. A new apartment in Nice, the cement still wet, the title as clear as a glass of Chardonnay, where is the fun in that? Whereas this, a complex vintage of mysterious provenance, so much more fun."

The table at which they were sitting was one of a half-dozen tables in the small café on the edge of the village of Cipières lodged in the bosom of Les Alpes Maritimes. There were only two cafés in the village and this was the one that had been there the longest, had opened in the immediate aftermath of the Second World War. The other, a long derelict building that had once housed *une forgerie*, had been opened barely three years ago by a couple from Antibes. The new owners had restored the building in local stone, and made of it an attractive cottage-style restaurant. But after three years they were still strangers, three years hardly counted at all in a village rooted in the Middle Ages, a village with a handful of family names repeated over and over in the shaded graveyard beside the plain white church.

The previous year, an article by a reporter from Antibes — 'just a girl' was how the villagers characterized her — about the great real estate deals in the area had appeared in one of the national weeklies. The young woman had taken a glass of Chablis at the café that was now named la vieille forgerie, and talked to the owners for as long as it took to finish the glass. She had described the village and, by inference the villagers, as charmingly primitive, and offering wonderful opportunities for city dwellers looking for country retreats. Some land and property had sold as a consequence. The beginning of change was in the air, like a chill blown in from the valleys to the north, although it was a chill that would not be felt by the real estate prospectors who stopped in at la vieille forgerie. There, the bucolic charms of the village and the rustic good neighbourliness of its plainspoken residents would be routinely extolled by the couple from Antibes, eager for more people like themselves to come with purses and wallets lined with plastic. Those who stopped at Le café, where Rufus and Jean-

Paul sat, would immediately feel the draught, through service even more indifferent than usual and looks chillier than the Chenin-Blanc. But Rufus' French was poor and Jean-Paul was a lawyer, so both were inured to chills.

The village was constructed exclusively out of the local stone that, like its older inhabitants, came in shades of speckled brown and pale grey. A hodgepodge of houses and apartments had grown almost organically over the centuries shaped and directed by the contours of the land. Without street names or numbers, it could be difficult to determine where one dwelling ended and another began. The lower third of the village was accessible only via a narrow bridge, walled on either side with blocks of stone an arm's-span wide. The thoroughfare between would permit one car at a time to cross, although a car and *un velo* could pass together. This river beneath the bridge was the runoff from the soaring, snow-covered peaks that cradled the sky. In the spring, it became a torrent, throwing up a light-bending mist as it leapt and splashed across the smooth brown stones of the riverbed. Some years before a child had fallen in and, further down at a bend in the river, a simple stone shrine with a plaster *vierge* marked the spot where the river had given up her small, drowned body. There were flowers at the shrine. Sometimes they were withered, sometimes they were fresh; but there were always flowers.

The main street continued across the bridge and ended in the upper village at a wide low wall made from blocks like those in the bridge. Scarring the faces of the stones were clichéd declarations of enduring love made by generations of sweethearts. Beyond the wall, the land dashed away precipitously, breathtakingly, to the valley floor a thousand feet below through the centre of which the river, a string of gleaming mercury, threaded its way. On this morning though, the river was hidden, the valley still shrouded in mist waiting to be burned off by the morning sun.

After bidding *adieu* to Jean-Paul, Rufus walked back along the cobbled street to where it opened into the small village square. Not that there was much open about the medieval square, hemmed in by various shapes and sizes of dwellings most with doors facing directly onto the cobbles of the square itself. He looked up to the sliver of red tile roof that sheltered his apartment, the topmost amidst the labyrinthine weave of different dwellings. Walking on, he came to the entrance to La Tabagie that stood at the corner. The small store sold everything from wine to shoe polish, and smelled of wine and herbs, centuries of varnished wood and, of course, tobacco. He stepped through the open doorway and into the shaded interior, nodding to the woman sitting behind the counter. He picked up the phone from the wall-bracket beside the door.

"*Londres, Angleterre, s'il-vous-plait.*" Rufus couldn't wait to tell Jenny that the deal was finally done. It had taken far longer than they had expected and, with prices in the area going up month to month, they were beginning to feel that something was going on and that they were going to have to pay more. In the end though, their fears had been unfounded and the delays just the nature of French bureaucracy. Now they owned — or at least were temporary custodians of — a little piece of France.

"Hello? Is that you Rufus?"

"Jen, hello, this bloody line . . . I can hardly hear you. Can you hear me, Jenny?"

"Yes, I can now. Is it done? Are we Mr. and Mrs. Blake of Cipières?"

"Actually no, we are Monsieur et Madame Blake de Cipières," replied Rufus with counterfeit pomposity.

"What a relief. I thought it would never happen. It's so exciting. When are you coming home?"

Rufus loved to hear his wife's voice, with her charming Home Counties lilt, unlike his own northern English with its flatter vowels and harder more angular edge. He could hear Adam and Ellie arguing over something in the background. Then suddenly there was a frozen silence, shattered by a great yowl as Adam burst into tears.

"Ellie, what did you do to Adam?" Jennifer asked, and then, "Adam come and show me."

Rufus, smiling as he eavesdropped on his children's minor tragedy, answered his wife's question, "I want to make sure everything is okay before I leave, and I want to speak to a couple of contractors about the well. I'll probably be back Friday."

"Darling I've got to go, these little horrors. Show Mummy darling." This was followed by a shuffling and sniffing, and Rufus waited patiently until the conversational ball ricocheted back in his direction. "Call me before you leave Rufus. That's too bad, Ellie, what have I told you about scratching? Come and say goodbye to Daddy, he's got to go."

"I don't want to," from Ellie in the distance.

"Adam, say goodbye to Daddy."

"Bye, Daddy. Daddy, Ellie scratched me. On the hand."

"Adam, it was probably an . . . "

"It wasn't, Daddy, she did it on purpose. She did it on purpose, Daddy . . . " Then more tears and shuffling of the phone, and finally just the buzzing of a disconnected line. Still smiling, shaking his head, Rufus replaced the handset in its cradle. Reaching into his pocket he withdrew a couple of coins, deposited them on the counter and, nodding again to the woman who had remained unmoving behind it, he ducked below the low lintel above the doorway and out into the sunshine.

There were two parts to the purchase: the apartment was the principal part; but along with it, because of some long-standing historical connection, they had also acquired an oddity — a small triangle of land located in the bottom third of the village beyond the river. On this patch of land was a well, albeit one that had been bone dry for as long as anyone could remember; also, as if to guarantee its redundancy, since the early forties when the Germans had occupied the country it had been filled in with rocks, earth, and rubble. Too small to do much with, this plot and its well, had remained unchanged in more than twenty years.

Rufus continued down the cobbled street toward the bridge. The early morning cool had now completely gone. Sweat tickled his armpits, and he removed his linen jacket and slung it across his shoulder. He looked up at the mountains glittering brilliantly against the flat blue sky. Jagged ridges and peaks of ice and snow towered in the north and east, then gradually fell away to more modest crests in the west and south, where the broad sweeping valleys led to the sea an hour-and-a-half's drive away.

When Rufus and Jenny had first come to the area, it had been as tourists. The children, Adam and Ellie, had made friends with the local doctor's son, and it was through that acquaintance that they had learned that the apartment was on the market. Dr Nathan Delalande and his wife Annette, also a doctor, were themselves relative newcomers. Annette was a researcher at the Clinique de Cancer in Cannes, but with their oldest just four years, and Annette having just given birth to their second, she was on an extended leave from the Clinique. They had arrived two summers ago with their son Marc and had conceived their second child, Chloe almost straight away. Perhaps the mountain air, the villagers had joked among themselves. Unlike many strangers, the Delalandes had been, if not quite welcomed, then at least guardedly acknowledged. Before Nathan had opened his practice, the villagers of Cipières and neighbouring villages had to travel to Antibes for medical attention, so a local doctor was a welcome arrival. But before the slow trickle of outsiders into the area, Nathan had found barely enough patients to support his practice. Now with the growing interest from outside the region, either from people on weekend getaways, or from young families who couldn't afford the prices on the coast, Nathan soon found himself busy enough. This was especially the case during the summer months because of the time it took to travel between the various communities to see his older patients.

As he walked, Rufus' cast his mind back to the first time he and Jenny had discussed their purchase of the apartment with Nathan and Annette. It had been only shortly after they had met the French couple who invited them for a glass of wine.

"It seems that the property has been unofficially for sale for a while by . . . how do you say it? *Annette, comment dit-on, selon des rumeurs?*"

"'Word of mouth' is what Nathan means," Annette said.

"Ah *oui*, word of the mouth," Nathan sat in a plastic patio chair downwind from the other three, his right elbow resting on the arm of the chair, a rumpled, unfiltered cigarette between the index and middle finger of his right hand. He was a tall, thin, long-limbed man who, with his arms and legs draped against the uprights and horizontals of the patio chair, looked all angles. Around forty and with a long nose and large brown eyes that seemed larger for being set in cadaverous features, he took a lungful of the richly-scented tobacco before continuing. "We have since learned why that might be, eh Netti?"

Wearing cotton shorts and T-shirt, Annette sat on another white patio chair, her knees pulled up in front of her. She continued the story. "When we first started to think about coming here, we heard about three places that might be right for us — here, of course, also the apartment that we'd heard could be bought, and the other was a place in Greolières, a village close to here. It turned out, though, that only this would do; it had to be big enough for our family and the practice." She changed position restlessly, pulling her knees sideways under her and looked across the patio to the small garden where her son Marc was playing with Adam and Ellie. All three children were intently examining something at the edge of the stone pathway where tall grass and shrubbery started. Their youngest, Chloe, was in a bassinette by her side.

"*Qu'est-ce-que vous avez trouvé, la, mes enfants?*" Annette had to raise her voice only slightly. The distance was not far and without the background clutter of urban life, the question carried easily in the clear mountain air. The children didn't even look up.

"She worries about snakes. Don't you, Netti?" said Nathan dryly.

Then Ellie called out, "Adam, don't."

But Adam wasn't to be deterred and continued to poke at something in the tall grasses. Alarmed at the word snakes, it was now Jennifer's turn to call out, a scratch of alarm in her voice, "Ellie, what's Adam got there?"

"I found a snail, Mummy, and Adam's poking it with a stick," Ellie cried out crossly.

The two women visibly relaxed and the men smiled, continuing to pretend they had never been concerned

"*Ou etais-je?*" said Annette. "Ah, *oui*. When we looked at the apartment, it was clear right away it would never do; but we were intrigued by the old well that went with it. Nathan even thought he might be able to build a small, er, clinic on the site and have the apartment separate, but it wasn't really practical. Anyway, then we looked at this place and, of course, it was big enough for both. I mean our family and the practice. It was more money, but we loved it right away," Annette looked at Nathan when she said this, and he smiled back.

"It's beautiful. I can see why you would," Jenny said, looking at the flowering clematis that crawled across the back of the house, the profusion of wild flowers bursting out of the window boxes below the shuttered windows, and from the halves of barrels that lined the patio where they sat.

"Of course, in a village four hundred or so years old, everything has a story, even this place," said Nathan. "But, Netti, go on, tell Rufus and Jenny the story." Nathan leaned forward with the dark bottle, "Rufus, your glass." Rufus slid his glass toward him. Annette and Jenny's glasses remained barely touched.

"Well," Annette started, "You know of course how it was in France after 1940? No, of course, how could you know, your 'sceptered Isle.' That's a line I remember, so beautiful. It was terrible when the Germans came into Paris with their grey uniforms and tanks. It seems like another lifetime ago

and I was very young, but I remember my mother crying."
Annette stopped and took a sip of her wine. "I was twelve
when the war ended, but it seemed to have lasted forever, it
was all I'd known. It was much worse for Nathan, of course."
She stopped again and looked across at her husband.

Nathan smiled, "My dear, you digress. She means I am
a Jew, and it was not a good time to be a Jew ... or a Pole,
a Gypsy, a Russian ... it was not a good time to be a lot of
things, the fascists were very egalitarian in their prejudices.
Nathan placed the glass of wine he had been holding onto
the table in front of him. "I, too, am from the north, not Paris
but a town called Melun, further south a little way. My father
was a doctor there, in the town. My mother taught piano *au
conservatoire* in Paris. She would go in twice a week on the
train, and sometimes she would take me with her. I was little
then, a child." Nathan picked up the packet of Gauloise. "I
used to love that, going into town with her, it felt so grown
up. Nathan paused, played with the cigarette packet that
he held in his hands. "My mother's name was Rebecca; my
father's name was Daniel. They died in Auschwitz."

Nobody spoke, and Nathan busied himself extracting a
cigarette from the packet, which he lit with his small metal
lighter. He took a couple of long inhalations then sat with
the cigarette held down between his legs. He smiled briefly,
"It is strange to find at twelve years of age, having been born
here and having lived all of your twelve years here, that you
are not as French as your neighbours, that you are Jewish
before you are French. It was our neighbours who betrayed
my family. It was not the Germans who sent my parents to
Auschwitz; it was the French police, *la Milice de Vichy*, our
own S.S. The last time I saw my parents, I was staying with
the family of one of my mother's students. My mother still

taught piano, no longer at a school — she was a Jew and no longer good enough — but privately. She had a small number that would come in the evenings. Some were very young, younger than me. I remember them coming in three or four evenings a week, carrying their little satchels, and the awful, stumbling, mechanical sound of their scales and exercises." Nathan smiled at the memory, inspecting the remainder of his cigarette as he did so.

"The little girl, the girl whose family I stayed with was named Natalie, Natalie Loutits. My parents and the Loutits had become not exactly friends, but something like that. When my parents could see what was happening, they sent me to stay with the Loutits. I didn't see my parents a lot after that. Anyway, I stayed with the Loutits after the war, until I went to medical school on a scholarship. The Loutits helped me, they were very good people. Perhaps also they felt guilty, not for themselves of course, but they had seen what had happened. I was lucky. I remember the last time I saw my parents. I remember saying goodbye in the hallway, my mother embracing me, my father as well, which was not like him. I expected to see them again of course, but they didn't come, they never did. Nathan took a final short puff on the cigarette before grinding it into the ashtray.

"That's awful," said Jennifer, her eyes brimming, "I'm so sorry."

Nathan picked up his wineglass. He looked up at Jennifer and smiled, "When I play piano I honour my mother. I became a doctor to honour my father. Medicine, it is an honest profession. Thank God he wasn't a lawyer, a whore to whoever has the money." Nathan smiled again, and offered by way of explanation, "I was a Marxist before I was a doctor."

"Ha, *mon cheri*, you are simply too old and too . . . comfortable to be a Marxist. Yes, Fidel is a doctor, but that is Cuba, this is France. You have never been a Marxist; you have just been a romantic. You are still a romantic; that is why I love you." Annette leaned across to Nathan and kissed him on the cheek.

"My wife is typical bourgeoisie. She comes from a privileged background so she knows that politics is just a game that the powerful play to confuse the poor, the poor who fail to see that the game is . . . how do you say it? Fixed? Anyway, forgive me my dear that we do not enter into this dialectic in front of our friends. We can do so later to inflame our passions, before we make love."

Annette smiled, and so did Rufus and Jennifer. "You're all talk, Nathan," said Annette.

"It is true that, sadly, I am no longer seventeen," replied Nathan, "Anyway, there is no passion without words; it is words which separate us from beasts."

"Perhaps humour," suggested Rufus

"You are right, Rufus, human sexuality is often a cause for humour," replied Nathan.

"Enough," said Annette, smiling, "enough. Nathan, you embarrass our guests."

"Aah, my wife is a prune I think," said Nathan as he took his wife's hand and kissed it with great tenderness.

Annette smiled indulgently, "Prune? I think you mean prude, *Cherie*."

"Ah yes, of course. Anyway, the war is long over now . . . Netti, why are we talking about the war?"

"The apartment," said Annette. "You were telling them about the apartment." She smiled at Jennifer. "I worry what he will be like when he gets old, if he's like this at forty."

"*Quarante-et-un ma cherie*," said Nathan.

"I will tell the story," Annette said. "But first, Jennifer, come with me, please. We will get the children something, I think, and something to have with the wine. Nathan *cheri, va verifier Chloe*," and, saying this, Annette took Jennifer's hand and led her inside.

"I never know what I'm supposed to do when she says that. The child is sleeping, no?" Nevertheless, Nathan stood up and walked over to the bassinette. He lifted the light cover that shielded his daughter from the sunlight and peered in. "*Ah petite Chloe. Tu es reveillée.* Now be a good girl and close your eyes again." Rufus could hear vague scrabbling and gasping, the strange little vocalizings of a six-month-old. "I think you are very optimistic, Nathan," he said.

"One can only hope, I suppose," Nathan replied.

Annette's voice carried through the kitchen window. "*Tu es impossible, Nathan, ta fille te veux comment peux-to vouloir qu'elle se rendort?*" Then in English to Jennifer, "I think doctors make the worst fathers. He treats her like something from outer space, like a lab specimen."

"You are too cruel, darling. It is easier for a woman, because babies need you. Rufus agrees, don't you Rufus." Nathan looked meaningfully at Rufus.

"We men are all as bad; it is a sad truth," Rufus said. Then, as if to further legitimize his support of Nathan, added, "Below twelve months, I've never thought children very interesting, even my own. Of course, I love them, but the fact is they are not very, well . . . compelling, involving? Before they, er, can participate in the world."

"*Oui, participer a la vie,* we are in accord my friend . . . " said Nathan in muted tones. "Especially other people's children, not friends' children of course, you understand, but children in general, in the shops and on the street that women ... how do you say, coo-coo over? I think, in England, fathers have nothing to do with the children, is that not so? Perhaps here it would be the same, but so many men here pretend differently. They give women the impression that men think little children are interesting, which is ridiculous, the brain has not yet fully developed."

Half an hour later, with the children sitting on the grass eating cake with a pitcher of pear juice between them, and the adults with a variety of breads, cheeses, olives, and fruits on the table, the conversation continued. Chloe was now nursing contentedly and Nathan had opened a second bottle of red wine, although this was now a local wine.

"That was an excellent Bourdeaux, thank you, Rufus, Jennifer. I hope you will think well of this little wine, this *Vin de Pays*, it is one of our favourites with lunch — from a little vineyard west of here. It is on very pleasant south-facing slopes with very ... you say, I believe, arid soil? Annette and I always fetch a case when we are over that way. It is not big at all and should be drunk quite soon, but it has very pleasant ... Annette, how do I say *nuances?*"

"Nuances," said Annette.

"Ah, *oui*, it is the same, *nuances*. I forget how much the English language owes to the French," and saying this Nathan poured out two fresh glasses for himself and Rufus. Jennifer's glass remained half-full and Annette was now drinking water. Nathan shook his head. "*Annette* thinks that wine is bad for Chloe while she is nursing. Ridiculous, of course, but I must respect her ... *sentiment?*"

"Intelligence," said Jennifer, abruptly.

"*Oui*, of course, that is what I mean," said Nathan who now lit another cigarette.

Annette smiled tartly, "You smoke too many of those, Nathan."

"You are right of course, my dear," replied Nathan.

Annette shook her head slightly. "So. The apartment." Annette had settled herself comfortably, a light shawl draped across her shoulder behind which Chloe's head was nestled against her breast. "I will tell the story. Nathan cannot tell a story unless you plan to be here until midnight."

"You make our guests feel unwelcome *cheri,* and I like to give a complete account."

Annette leaned forward and started to speak, "So you know, of course, of *Vichy France*? Of course you do. The south of the country was Vichy, the north was occupied France. It was not good, but at least Vichy was under French governance; they were not the Germans. Of course, once the Germans took over, which they did after the Allies landed in '43 and the Italians collapsed, then it became different — much more like the occupied zone. The Germans came and just took over whatever buildings they wanted and installed their officers, mostly in the good homes and especially those with good wine cellars. Villages like this had no strategic value, not like the towns with ports on the coast, but the Maquis became more active, especially in the mountains. You have probably heard of the stories, and everyone has heard of Lidice?" Annette looked at Rufus and then at Jennifer.

"The village in Poland?" said Rufus.

"Exactly," continued Annette, "where, after their resistance killed the German headman — his name was . . . er . . . I think, Heydrich, yes, Reinhard Heydrich — the Germans killed every man, woman and child in the village, or they sent them to the camps which was the same thing, and then burned the village to the ground, erased it from history."

"Except, of course, they didn't. Now everyone has heard of Lidice." Nathan drew another draft of smoke into his lungs. "But, of course, the men, women and children are just as dead. They didn't want to become some historical reference point in the history of man's evil, just to live their lives. How do you say it in English, in that very vulgar way? Fucking Germans? Not Nazis — that was just a political party. This was not a war between political parties — the Nazis versus the Third Republic, the Nazis versus your Conservative Party or your Labour Party. It was the English, the French, the Germans. It was Germans who were often also Nazis, but it was still Germans. And then, at Nuremburg, when the bastards were brought to account, they said they were acting on orders. Phhh!" Nathan spat his contempt. "Of course, logically, such consequences are effective — support for resistance diminishes when resistance actions lead to such awful consequences as Lidice. And Germans are very logical." Nathan smiled thinly. "There was a German officer billeted in the village ... "

"You see?" said Annette, "After an excursion into the political map of Europe we get to it."

"The context is important, my dear," said Nathan.

Ignoring her husband, Annette began. "So, this German in the village. He was they say ... "

"Who are 'they'?" asked Rufus

"Oh, people here, the villagers," Nathan answered, "I am their doctor, some of the older people want to talk." Nathan's words carried on a pillow of smoke. "He was, they say, young, and a typical German. You know, blond, blue-eyed, good looking and charming. Charming, of course, unless you were Jewish."

"Are there still bad feelings here about Germans?" Rufus asked.

"This is only twenty or so years ago, I think there are bad feelings about the Germans everywhere in Europe. And this is a small community, a close community, they have long memories, time stands still in places like this, twenty years ago is yesterday," said Nathan.

"Anyway," Annette again picked up the thread, "remember that all of this area was part of Vichy, France. Even though the Germans had taken over, it was still something like that, that is that the people of the south had an *entente*, an accord with the Germans. But villages like this one have their own views, and anyway it was in the mountains that the Maquis had their hiding places." Annette paused to take a sip of water and then said, "The rumour that we have heard is that one of the girls in the village, a young girl, sixteen or so was, not in love, but a young person's idea of love, *entiche*?"

"Smitten?" said Rufus.

"Infatuated," said Jennifer.

"Ah, *oui*, infatuated, I think," said Annette.

"You know Michel, *le boulanger*?" Nathan asked.

"Yes, of course," said Jennifer, "we buy our bread there — there is nowhere else. But, I would not say we know him. He is quite, er, taciturn," and seeing the look of puzzlement on Annette's face, Jennifer added, "He doesn't say much."

"Ah *oui*," said Annette, the cloud of incomprehension suddenly lifting, "He does not say much and that is, how you say it, taciturn? That is not a word I have heard before."

"Forgive me, Annette. You and Nathan have such excellent English I forget sometimes that it is not your language." Jennifer leaned forward and picked up her glass.

"Well . . ." Annette began, "this girl that was *entiche*, infatuated with the German, was Michel's sister, his twin sister. He has another sister who is older than him and, in fact, we have seen her — she was visiting him earlier this year. The other sister, this twin, we have never seen."

"She left the village?" asked Rufus.

Annette gave a slight shrug, "She left? Perhaps. She eloped with her soldier boyfriend? Maybe. She was thrown out? It has been suggested."

Any of these things are possible. We don't know but we have heard rumours, bits and pieces." Nathan interjected.

Annette spoke again, "It would have been shameful for her family to have a daughter spending time with the German officer, but she was young and he also was young, handsome, and in uniform and, maybe in her mind, an ally. After all, who knows how a young girl in love thinks? She doesn't. And it seems this German was always finding ways to come to the house, to bring things that were difficult to get in those days. More than once he took her and her brother into Antibes or to Nice in his car, or went fishing with the boy down at the river. Maybe he was lonely for his own family. Maybe he just wanted to be a part of their family in a way, who knows, but it seems he was very persistent. This was I believe in 1943, I don't know for sure, maybe earlier." Annette paused and had another sip of her water before continuing. "But it would have made things very difficult you can see?"

"I have heard how, at the end of the war, women and girls who had been 'friendly' with Germans were tarred and feathered, heads shaven, beaten if they were lucky," said Rufus.

"Yes of course, this was war, the Germans were occupiers," said Nathan.

"Anyway, we are told that her father, Michel's father, he died many years ago by the way, was very unhappy at this German's attentions to his family, but what could he do? He was a vassal in his own country, his own home."

"What about their mother?" asked Jennifer.

"There was only their father. Their mother died giving birth to the twins. They were raised by their father," said Nathan.

"So what have these rumours been?" Rufus asked.

Annette answered, although her gaze was on the children playing in the grasses, "The girl, Michel's sister, disappeared and at the same time so did the young German officer. Immediately the Germans came looking for him but there was no trace. That he was often at the house was well-known to his comrades. They searched the house, scoured the area and could find nothing. The Germans were very suspicious and did not, at first, believe that their man would run away from his post with a French girl. But there was no soldier and no French girl. So it seemed the only thought, the only conclusion that could be made was that they had run away together."

"That's so romantic, that they ran away together; among all that horror, there was love," said Jenny.

"They just disappeared?" asked Rufus.

"It seemed so, to the Germans anyway," replied Nathan enigmatically.

"We have never really got a clear answer to what happened and there are people in the village who know for sure," said Annette.

"You mean they have never been back? They just disappeared?" asked Jennifer

"Would that not have been dangerous for her?" asked Rufus.

Nathan looked up, "Perhaps. In the north, yes, but she was very young, sixteen, maybe younger? Also, you must again remember that there was cooperation with the Germans. Even in the north many people cooperated and, although as a Frenchman I am ashamed to say it, many people believed that the little corporal's policies toward Jews, toward my people, were the right ones. Anti-Semitism is only a little below the surface in this country. Our own government, *le gouvernement de Vichy*, was so enthusiastic to have the *Statuts des Juifs*, the anti-Jewish laws, proclaimed; even now I sometimes wonder why I am still here."

"The thought was occurring to me," said Rufus.

Nathan shrugged. "I am a Jew, but I am also French, as were the Loutits who took me in at great risk to themselves. This is my language; this is my country. Anyway, forgive me. This story has nothing to do with Jews." Nathan leaned forward and ground his cigarette into the overflowing ashtray.

"Sorry, Nathan, I know I can be a bit obtuse. That it has nothing to do with Jews I accept, but what has this got to do with the apartment?" asked Rufus.

Nathan looked surprised, "The apartment? Oh nothing at all really. Except that when you buy the apartment, you also buy the well."

"The well?"

"Yes, the well, Rufus, the well that is filled with rocks my friend."

"Yes, I know that the purchase includes the small piece of land with the well . . . "

At this point Jennifer pitched in. "Nathan, you were telling us about the girl and the German soldier that she was infatuated with and they have never been back."

"Jennifer, I am sorry, you are right, Annette is quite right, I digress, and yes, they have never been back, but then it was wartime, it was chaos and confusion." Nathan fumbled in his jacket pocket until he brought out a crumpled cigarette packet and lit yet another cigarette before continuing. "You must remember, as I said, we know only what the people here want us to know. I am their doctor, not their confessor, although I admit, sometimes I think I am that as well. But this young German was seen much in the village and, as I said, he was often seen at the house of Michel and his sisters. No doubt this young man, like all young men, would have boasted to his comrades about making love with the beautiful young French girl. I have heard that she was beautiful and perhaps she was; a beautiful girl can turn any man from his duty. Of course beauty can often also be a fiction, invoked in a tale to lend some tragedy to it, as though the misfortunes of the plain and ugly must be less tragic, and perhaps more deserved, by their ugliness. Humanity is so shallow. She may have been just a plain child, *une villageoise,* but the legend insists that she was beautiful. Whatever the truth, the Germans . . . Netti *comment dit-on?*"

"Reluctantly," said Annette.

"*Oui,* reluctantly, they believed that is what happened, that their young officer had run away with this beautiful French girl. After all, that she was beautiful would make it more believable, no? Had they not believed that they had run away, there might have been, Netti, *comment des mauvaises consequences?*

"Not good consequences," said Annette.

"Of course, how stupid am I, bad consequences." There was a brief silence.

"Nathan, I'm confused. You are saying that the Germans believed that this young man ran off with Michel's sister, but you are not saying that he did? You are not saying something?" Jenny wrinkled her brow.

Nathan was once more wreathed comfortably in smoke. "No one speaks about it, Jennifer. As I said, we have only heard bits and pieces, often contradictory, but what we are led to believe is this. There were those in the village who were with the Maquis, and the rumour we have heard is that the Maquis gave her father no choice, he was to send her away, to another country, maybe Switzerland, I don't know. Then they killed the German and, of course, had to be sure the body would not be found. They could not afford to have the body found. Even without a body, the Germans could have taken men from the village and shot them, just on suspicion — they didn't need proof. But if they had found the body it would have been certain."

"I think I understand," said Rufus tonelessly.

"What! What are you saying, Rufus, understand what?" said Jenny.

"Sweetheart . . ." began Rufus.

"It is just a rumour," said Nathan. "No one knows for sure, but the girl is sent away, the German disappeared, the well was filled with stone." Nathan looked at Annette. "Netti, *Des evenements contemporains oui, mais contigus? Qui sait?*"

"Did the one thing touch on the other, I think is what Nathan means," said Annette.

"Oh no!" said Jenny looking appalled. "They didn't run away together? Oh no. You mean? You mean two children fall in love and one is banished and the other killed? His body in our well? No. That's awful. That's too awful."

"It was not two children, Jenny. It was one child perhaps. The other was a German officer, no matter what his age, no matter how beautiful he was. That is war, Jenny. There is nothing good in war," said Nathan.

"But we don't know for sure? You say this is just a rumour Nathan." said Jenny "They could still have run away together."

"It's possible," said Annette. "Everything is rumour but you can see that it was very important that the Germans believed that they had run away together."

"I think it probable that they did," said Rufus, adding, "but I don't understand why this other thing is still a rumour. It was twenty years ago. That, as you say Nathan, is not such a long time. Surely the people here must know one way or another; the men who are supposed to have done it must know and, anyway, the war is long gone. There is no need for secrecy. The Germans were occupiers; if it happened, it was an act of resistance — patriotism, not murder. Surely if there was a body it would have been recovered by now and returned to Germany? Like Bob Dylan says, 'now we're all friends, with God on our side,' or something like that."

Annette looked at Rufus, "You must remember, as Nathan said, we, too, are new here. There are things we do not know yet and may never know. It is a village with, until very recently, no one from the outside. Even the priest is from the village. He grew up here and he, too, was with the resistance we have heard. Then after the war, he took holy orders, I think you say that, took orders? Went into a seminary, became a priest. Then he returned here. That is uncommon, I think, in the priesthood to come back to your home." Annette paused, then added, "It is a very tight community. Look at the names on the gravestones, you will see what I mean."

"Look on the bright side." Nathan said, smiling, "The apartment is very attractive with a superb view and the price is good. Yes, the well becomes yours also, but for the rest? We will never know. The well is filled with stone and the growth of twenty years. *Mon amis*, I'm a Jew, I know good value. Buy the apartment; just leave well alone. Ah! A pun I believe?"

The rain came down with a steady roar, sluicing off the shiny black-slate roofs of the houses of the village of Chipping Norton. Rufus stood before the open windows looking out into the darkness, breathing in the smell of the rain-drenched countryside, listening to the sound of water gurgling in the pipes and gutters. The children were finally asleep. Jennifer was curled up on the sofa behind him, a glass of Chardonnay on the table beside her.

"If they didn't run away together, if the Resistance killed the German, it wasn't really murder, you know; it was war. It was a different time. A lot of people died but it wasn't murder in the way we mean that. Now it seems cold blooded, but I mean you know what the Nazis did to Nathan's parents and to millions of others." But Rufus knew his wife, knew how she would respond even as the words left his lips.

"How can you talk like that, Rufus? He was just a boy, a boy who fell in love with a girl. And no one has said he was a Nazi — just a soldier, a boy, just a boy. The Wermacht were not necessarily Nazis. You men, and your gangs and your tribes — so stupid, so childish and so awful."

"Well, there's a bit more to it than that, sweetheart. I mean Nazi Germany was a bit more than just a tribe. And Hitler's Brownshirts and his Waffen SS, a bit more than just gangs. I mean, you know, a bit more than just that."

"I don't want to quibble, Rufus. I will not live in a place with some poor murdered boy's body in it — I will not!"

"Sweetheart, what do you want me to do, dig the whole thing up? And anyway, the apartment is not the well. It's completely separate. We needn't ever even go there."

"Yes, that's exactly what I want."

"To just not go there?"

"Rufus, you know what I mean. You must dig it up and if this boy's body is there then it should be returned to his family, if they are still alive. Isn't that what you would want? What if it was our son? What if it was Adam?"

Christ! Thought Rufus. "Sweetheart . . ." he began

"Rufus, I'm serious, you have to promise me that you'll do it or I'll never go there. You have to promise."

Rufus continued to look out into the night, thinking that he loved Oxfordshire, its scents, the soft-edged glory of its glades, sheep-dotted pastures and round-humped hills, wondering did they really need a place in France, did he need all this shit? But nevertheless, he promised.

The original circular wall of the well was still two-thirds intact. The other third had disappeared into the ground, much of it beneath a now fair-sized tree that had moulded its roots up and over the remains of the well, grown over it like history. The interior of the well was completely overtaken by nature, the rocks and stone lost beneath grass, shrub and moss.

There was only one man in the area, Claude, who might have had the equipment to do the job. During one of the several trips across to France that Rufus had made during the time it took to bring the purchase to that morning's conclusion, Rufus had met with him and explained what he wanted.

"So, Claude, will you do it? When we get down to where the body is supposed to be, if there is a body, I'll take over. I'll contact the German Consulate and invite them to complete the recovery."

Claude didn't even pause to consider. "I'm too busy and anyway the site is inaccessible. I don't think you should even attempt it. The best thing is to leave it alone."

"I should have mentioned that I am an architect. Believe me it should be quite straightforward," Rufus rejoined, nettled that Claude should be so dismissive of his suggestion.

"*Et je suis un excavateur.* And anyway, as I said, I'm too busy," Claude snapped.

"All right. Can you then suggest someone who might do the job?" Rufus asked.

"No. If the German is there, he has been there a quarter of a century. You haven't been here at all. There are strong feelings in the village. We don't want Germans coming here again. You should leave some things alone." Claude then added, "If you dig up the well, you dig up the past. That is why it has never been touched. If you want to build there, then fill it in with concrete. That's what we should have done years ago; that would be best."

"I agree that would be a solution. But it's not so simple," said Rufus, thinking of Jenny. "That wouldn't work."

In the course of a couple more visits, Rufus had tried, without success, to find a local contractor who would do the job. Furthermore, it became quickly apparent that his plans for the well had become common knowledge and the subject was raised often, whether he was taking a glass of wine at the old café where he'd been grudgingly accepted for his loyalty, or buying bread at the only bakery in the village, the bakery owned by Michel.

"*Bonjour,* Monsieur Blake."

"*Bonjour,* Michel, please call me Rufus. I'll have *une* baguette, please, and maybe a half-dozen of those *petits pains aux olives noires.*"

"I hear you are thinking of digging up the well, Monsieur *Blake.*" Rufus estimated that Michel was in his mid to late thirties. He was of a slight build, not the stereotypical plump baker, a hundred forty pounds at most. And his voice went with his build, having a mellifluous quality to it that further enhanced a language that needed no enhancing.

"We're planning to, yes," said Rufus a little uncertainly. He heard the door open and close behind him. "The war was a long time ago and we thought maybe, if there is a body there, if this German soldier's body is there, to return the remains to his family — if he has any. We think it would be the right thing to do. We are all on the same side now it seems and anyway to be quite honest, we don't like the idea of a body on our land, no matter how long it has been there."

Michel looked at him across the counter. "The German soldier? I have heard that rumour too. It is just a rumour. The well hasn't been touched in twenty years. We, that is, we villagers prefer that it should stay untouched. *Es-tu d'accord mon père?*" This was addressed to the man who had come in behind Rufus, who turned then to acknowledge him.

"*Bonjour,* Father," said Rufus who despite himself gave a respectful nod as he spoke. He also quickly appraised the man. The priest was older than Michel by perhaps a decade, but lean and dark with sharp, intense features and dark-brown eyes that seemed almost black. He wore the traditional beret, a black cotton shirt and white collar under a dark jacket, and dark corded pants held up by a wide leather belt. He inclined his head a degree by way of returning the greeting and, although the question had come from Michel, the priest looked at Rufus when he replied.

"Certainly it should not be touched. It is *un monument,* a memorial of a bad time in our history. What is done, if indeed anything was done, is done. What is buried, should remain buried." The priest spoke with the habit of authority. He was not giving an opinion, but an instruction.

"Will that be all, Monsieur Blake?" Michel said as he passed the bag of bread and plucked the proffered bank note.

Rufus looked at him. He could see how this man's sister might have been beautiful. Under close-cropped hair his features were clean and regular, and his skin clear and tight across high cheekbones. "I'm sorry if what I'm doing is hurtful for you, Michel, if it brings up painful memories of your sister, I truly am, but we cannot just pretend not to know." Rufus paused, but Michel said nothing and so Rufus persisted, "You were here. You've lived in this village all your life. You must know why the well was filled in. Is there a body in there or not? Somebody must be able to tell us."

"It was dry. It was dry and a danger to the children of the village," said the priest.

"So, there is no body of a German officer?" retorted Rufus.

"It was, as I say, a long time ago. Many of us in these villages were young men in those days, some of us with the Resistance, the Maquis, often had to be away. It was wartime; there are always mysteries and things that can never be completely known in war — sometimes not until long after — sometimes never."

"Well this is a mystery that can be easily solved. I intend to excavate the well," said Rufus firmly.

"You are young, Monsieur Blake. We lived through the war, some of us. One man from this village was executed by the Germans. I was, myself, with the Resistance in those years. It was after the war that I took holy orders. You English have . . . forgive me . . . you have no understanding of what it is like to be invaded — well, not since we invaded you much earlier, 1066, I think." The priest smiled when he said this. Michel looked down with the hint of a smile at the corners of his mouth. The priest said, "Trust me, Monsieur, it would be better to fill this well in completely, with concrete."

Rufus was starting to feel a little pressure and a little irritation. "You're not the first person to suggest that, Father." He took the bag and the change and turned to go, then added, "Thanks for your suggestions. I'll talk it over with my wife." As soon as the words were out of his mouth, he regretted saying them. Now, if they went ahead with the excavation, which he was more than ever determined to do, it would look as though Jenny had been the difficulty. "Bonjour, Monsieur Blake," said Michel without expression.

Rufus nodded "Good morning, Michel, Father."

The priest nodded briefly in return, and gestured farewell. Rufus noted the strong muscular fingers, one of which was adorned with a large jewelled ring. With a sigh of relief, Rufus stepped out onto the road.

That night he called Jenny. "You wouldn't believe what's happening here, Jen. I mean I feel like the whole village is on our case because of the well — even the damn priest. It's like the goddamned Mafia"

"What do you mean?"

"This whole thing of maybe a dead German being down there. I don't understand it, but it's aroused some strong feelings. No wonder the place hasn't been touched in twenty-odd years. Michel and the priest, they must know but they're not saying."

"You know how I feel about it, Rufus," said Jennifer. "I want to believe there is nothing there, that they ran away together, but I have to know. I won't live there not knowing. I mean it."

So finally, Rufus arranged for Gilbert from Antibes to come out and look at the job, and arranged to meet with him the morning after the final exchange of title with Jean-Paul. That evening Rufus returned to the *pension* where he'd rented a room for the weekend. He took a bottle of the local red to his room and fell asleep in the chair. Uncomfortable and dozing fitfully, his dreams were populated by German storm troopers and caricatured beret-topped members of the Maquis. Among the faces of the latter, he recognized the priest, the baker, and Philippe from the old café. He couldn't sleep so he went out and bought a second bottle. He didn't remember finishing that one, just as he didn't remember taking off his clothes and crawling into bed.

Saturday morning Rufus awoke early as usual, although not as clear-headed as he might have liked. He looked at his watch, 6:15 AM. He was meeting Gilbert at 7:30. Like most builders, Gilbert's days started early. So when, after his shower and a pastry-and-coffee breakfast, Rufus turned the corner, he saw Gilbert's pickup already parked adjacent to the narrow well site.

"*Bonjour*, Gilbert, I hope I haven't kept you waiting?"

Gilbert shrugged and dropped a half-smoked cigarette into the dirt, grinding it briefly under the toe of his boot. "It is of no matter."

The two men walked up to the old well. There was nothing much to see. Rufus had explained everything to Gilbert when they'd met in Antibes. Gilbert held a long roll of paper in his hand.

"I am not surprised the well is dry. This was a shallow well and you have to go very far down for water in this area. That is why this village and the others here get their water piped in from the reservoir above Grasse."

"So you can do the job?" asked Rufus.

"Of course. If you are sure you wish it."

"Oh yes, I am sure I wish it. In fact, the sooner the better. But why do you say that?"

"You have to live here, not me. I live in Antibes. It's not like living in a village like this. Villages like this, they live in an earlier time," replied Gilbert, lighting another Caporal and throwing the match over the remains of the well wall.

"I think they will be happy when it's done. Really, how can they like living with this morbid possibility, a reminder of such a terrible time for their country?" asked Rufus.

Gilbert was young, like Rufus, in his early thirties. "I spoke to my father about this. He lives in Nevers, where I was born. He was in the Resistance during that time. I remember it myself, although I was only young, eight or nine years." Gilbert looked at Rufus, his eyes squinting through a veil of blue smoke. "He says there appear to have been many more people in the Resistance, once the war ended, than he ever knew about while the war was going on."

"Sorry, I'm not sure I follow," Rufus said letting his puzzlement show.

Gilbert looked at the cigarette he was holding between thumb and forefinger. "He said that the south was not known much for its resistance, that the Nazis were comfortable here."

"Well, anyway, it seems that in this village, at least, there were people who resisted, which is why I have this problem now," Rufus answered, somewhat defensively.

The excavation started on a sunny June morning. In order to avoid antagonizing the village, Rufus had arranged for a representative from the Allied War Graves Commission to be on hand, rather than someone from the German consulate. His name was Gordon Palmer, from Leeds, England who, despite his middling years, boasted a full mop of blond hair and had blue eyes the colour of topaz. He may as well have been German for all the villagers knew. Nathan, of course, had volunteered his help, an offer Rufus had gratefully accepted. By about midday, Gilbert had removed the last large piece of stone with his excavator. Rufus paid him cash and, when the four men returned from lunch, Gilbert wished Rufus luck and then loaded the large, red, tracked machine onto its low-loader and set off back to Antibes. Throughout the afternoon the three men took turns working in the cramped space, removing by hand, the smaller pieces of rock and masonry and, finally, trowels-full of dirt. It took longer than Rufus had expected, and their progress was observed by a steady trickle of villagers who came to watch, usually staying twenty minutes or so before deciding they had better things to do.

In the street, unfettered by any clock, children played in the warm afternoon sunshine.

Nathan was in the pit when he raised his hand "I have something." He put down the trowel and, reaching into his pocket, pulled out a pair of surgical gloves and put them on. Rufus and Gordon, who had been watching from perches on the pile of broken masonry and feeling rather redundant, stood up and moved closer. Leaning forward, Nathan began to scrape away the soil and gradually something smooth and white began to emerge. Rufus sat down on his heels to get a closer look.

"It's a skull, Rufus," said Nathan.

"God, I suppose I was hoping we wouldn't find anything," said Rufus as he peered intently at the partially-revealed object, "It's small, Nathan, is that all we are under all this flesh?"

"No. It is small," Nathan answered. He continued to brush away the earth and the white skull, patched with mud and dirt, was more clearly revealed.

"One of their boy soldiers?" asked Rufus while thinking it was just as Jen had suggested.

"It could be," interjected Gordon. "The Germans used many very young soldiers toward the end — children really — raised in the Hitler Youth, not even as big as their rifles."

"Perhaps," said Nathan, "or just a less than Herculean member of the master race. I don't know. Tell you the truth, I don't think I've really examined a skeleton since medical school." Nathan continued to brush away the dirt, then paused to tug gently at a shard of faded, filmy, light-blue fabric from the soil. He looked at it quizzically before laying it on the ground beside him. He picked up the brush again but continued to gaze at the piece of fabric. "In fact, it was not a whole skeleton. I was on a scholarship; I could afford only a half skeleton. I had to assume that the body is symmetrical, which fortunately for my patients, it is."

"Here, let me take a turn," said Rufus.

"Yes, of course," said Nathan "but just a moment, there is something . . . "

The moment grew to twenty minutes as under Nathan's steady brushing the earth was forced to relinquish its clasp on the rest of the remains. Rufus and Gordon continued to watch intently and quietly until finally Gordon broke the silence.

"I'm surprised that there is no trace of a uniform, not even buttons or buckles. It couldn't have decayed so completely, I wouldn't have thought."

"Burned, I would guess," said Rufus, "Fear of discovery, I suppose."

"It's possible," said Nathan coming to his feet. He looked up to Rufus holding out the brush, handle first and, as he did so, a small section of earth and detritus slid away from under the legs of the corpse he had just finished exposing. The sound echoed and Nathan was reminded that he was, after all, standing in a well, shallow or not, with no guarantee that he was as close to the bottom as he might like. He stepped quickly to a more substantial looking footing amidst the broken rocks, wood, and debris.

Rufus came to his feet, looking beyond Nathan into the site.

Nathan, once he was assured he was on a sound footing, turned to look. "*Mon Dieu!*"

"What is it?" asked Gordon whose view was obstructed by Nathan. And then, "Ahh," when he could see what the other two could see.

Where the debris had broken away, a rough piece of timber could be seen supporting the body and offering some protection to a narrow cavity beneath. From that cavity, relatively free of debris, a second skull now glared out at them.

"Christ," said Rufus.

"I don't believe so," Nathan said. "However, there is something else, my friends. It was puzzling me and it is possible that I am mistaken but I would say that the, er, remains of the first skeleton, well . . ." Nathan left what he had been about to say unsaid and having recovered his composure after the discovery of this second skeleton, immediately crouched down again, peered intently into the newly revealed space and, probing the dirt with his fingers, closed them over something small.

"What are you thinking, Nathan? What is that? What did you find?" Rufus asked.

Nathan answered without turning around, "Rufus, I cannot be sure. I am a doctor, yes, but as I say, I have hardly looked at a skeleton since medical school. The skull is small but then so are many men." Now he leaned back and looked again at the first skeleton and then at the small thing he held in his hand, "I think we should not assume that this is the remains of a man."

"A woman? The girl?" Rufus interjected.

"My friend, I do not know for sure, but I think it is not a young German Oberleutant. He would be in his twenties, probably of good build, a better build than us inferior Jews," Nathan smiled and held up his hand, palm upwards, "and he would have buttons like these on his tunic. This second body I think we can conclude is our handsome young German. No, this other skeleton was a small person, I would guess fifty, sixty kilos, no more, unless they were fat — but then who was fat in France in those days? An Aryan child? A Jewish woman? The irony is we are all the same at the grave. There is no *uber* race. But millions died because a handful of people thought so. If I were to guess?" Nathan picked up a thin stick and held it loosely, "A young person, a young woman, a girl maybe. Contrary to popular belief, there is no quick and certain way to determine sex from a skeleton. The differences are subtle, the variables many, and the areas of overlap considerable." Nathan pointed with the stick to the area above the eye sockets. "Sometimes a clue can be had here, above the orbits, but it is not conclusive. Just height and bone size are again clues but, likewise, not conclusive. The pelvic girdle is a strong indicator but I cannot clearly see, the way we are here. But if I had to guess, I think a young French girl who thought she was in love with a young German officer. Look at the remnant of clothing, not German army issue, I think. Cause of death? I don't know. It's impossible to tell." Nathan shuffled over and squatted next to the skull of the first skeleton. He pointed with the stick to the top of the spinal column. "See the vertebrae, how they are disturbed here. From the drop into the well? From the rocks and rubbish thrown on the bodies? Perhaps. Or from strangulation. From a very powerful man. It would have to be a man, no damage to the vertebrae like that would be possible from a woman. Ah, but what do I know, I'm a G.P. not a forensic pathologist"

The three men looked at each other.

"Our young lovers did not go very far," said Rufus.

"War," said Gordon, "what it makes of us." And then after a pause, "I think we have to call *Les Flics*." He pushed himself to his feet, and stretched, his hands holding the small of his back. "Is there a phone somewhere I can use?"

"There is a phone in the square, beyond the bridge," said Nathan, looking up. "I think we should wait here, Rufus." Nathan climbed up from the well. He looked across the road at a couple of village children who sat on a low wall. He didn't say anything, but pulled out his crumpled cigarette packet, extracted a familiarly rumpled cigarette, and lit it with his small lighter.

"Yes," said Gordon, "I will be a few minutes only." He started toward the small blue Renault parked at the curb then paused, "There's no hurry, not after twenty years. I'll walk." He set off along the cobbled street, his figure making long shadows in the evening sunlight.

Rufus and Nathan looked at each other.

"I don't think we can do much more now," said Nathan, sinking to his haunches, looking down into the well, inhaling slowly, and letting the smoke out in long, contemplative exhalations. The two children dawdled away. It was early evening, but the sun's warmth still leaked from the cobbles and the stone walls of the buildings. The village was quiet.

"Mmm," said Rufus turning to look as two figures, one bulky, one slight, turned the corner walking slowly until they arrived at the site. Rufus watched them look into the remains of the well and what it held. The baker showed no expression when his eyes met Rufus', but he sank soundlessly to his knees in the dirt and rubble, and covered his face with his hands. The priest made the sign of the cross, then placed his hand on the baker's shoulder.

Rufus reached out a hand but didn't touch Michel who, with his hands to his face, was looking over the tops of his fingers into the well. "I'm so very sorry, Michel. I had no idea. I didn't expect this. I thought your sister had been sent . . . I'm so sorry."

Pulling his hands down completely from his face, Michel inhaled deeply. "You don't understand, Monsieur, you don't understand at all."

The priest patted Michel's shoulder, "Ssh, Michel, ssh. "

Michel continued to look ahead when he spoke. "I am not the person you think I am, Monsieur. It was not me the German wanted, it was my brother."

Rufus heard the comment without at first understanding. When he did, he turned slowly, in confusion, to look at Michel. He saw again Michel's fine features, the slim frame and the slender fingers, now laced and resting on his knees.

"My God," he whispered .

The priest spoke softly. "The boy went against God and he went against his own people."

Rufus gazed at Michel and finally asked, "But why . . . ?

Still kneeling and without looking up Michel spoke, "Did you know, Monsieur, that my brother and I were twins?"

Rufus nodded, "I was told."

"My brother, Monsieur Blake, my brother was a beautiful boy, too beautiful you might say. The German officer, Norbert, he was handsome, blond, typical Aryan of course. An occupier yes, but he was courteous, and he was good to us. He was every young woman's dream. I was a girl. I was I think you say, infatuated, no? I was sixteen and even in war, love is all a sixteen-year-old girl thinks about. And he was not so much older than me — behind the uniform not much more than a boy, in the way all men are. And my brother? He idolized him, of course, and why not? Norbert was an officer in the most powerful army in the world and my brother was a boy. He let him drive his car, bought him presents, bought us presents. My father hated it, hated how easily he bought our affection, but he drank the coffee and he ate the chocolate. Understand, Monsieur, the Germans were resented of course, but not much resisted. Our neighbours, too. When they came to the house, they knew what they were putting in their mouths. They knew where it came from. Of course, everyone assumed I was his interest. At first, I thought that too. I was vain enough. But I never was. Pretty enough, perhaps? Hah! How wrong could I be! I never was his interest." Michel paused and for the first time looked up at Rufus. "My brother and I are . . . were, very close. I knew his mind before he knew it himself. I saw the way he looked at the German, the way glances and movements and gestures passed between them, betrayed them. Can you understand what I felt Monsieur? I was appalled, at first in disbelief, then when I realized — I was appalled and disgusted, and I hated my brother and the German equally."

The priest said something quickly to Michel, something that neither Rufus nor even Nathan caught. Michel looked up at the priest and smiled, "No, my dear friend, I want to tell it." Then, looking once more at the exposed secret of the well, Michel continued. "When suspicion grew into certainty, that their friendship was more than it seemed, that it was an unnatural relationship, yes — I suppose you would say that — then I became . . . something hateful, jealous, humiliated of course, especially humiliated, all those things." Michel shrugged and looked across at Nathan. "Doctor, would you mind, for my health?"

Nathan smiled and passed a cigarette, then taking his lighter from his pocket, leaned across and lit it. "When the unnatural is so commonplace, Michel, it hardly deserves to be called unnatural. What is imposed by nature and what is constructed by man is not the same thing."

Michel let out a long exhalation of the scented smoke, "Thank you, Doctor. Was my brother . . . seduced . . . by him? Was he seduced by my brother? I don't know, but youth alone is no guarantee of innocence, and if love in any of its forms is ultimately understandable, explainable at least, betrayal never is. He betrayed our people to him, to the German . . . it was I who discovered it and it was I who . . . "

" . . . told us," the priest completed.

" . . . who was painfully eager to tell the Resistance," Michel continued.

"It was the only right thing to do, Michel," said the priest.

"I agree," Michel responded, "and I would do the same again, but only because it would be the right thing to do, not because I wanted to, not with the same . . . enthusiasm."

"Yes, you said you were with the resistance," said Rufus, looking over at the priest.

"Of course, Monsieur, I led the cell in this area."

"He was just sixteen; he was a boy," said Rufus softly.

"So was my nephew, Monsieur, a boy who ran messages for us. The German's executed him . . . .eventually. He told them nothing."

Michel looked up at Rufus. "The Germans had to believe that their man had run away with me, and so . . . a haircut, a few changes. Even our names were the same. My given name was Michelle, the feminine of Michel. Not so difficult, eh? "

"Mmm," said Rufus

"You disappeared, but never left their sight," said Nathan.

"I suppose I understand. I mean, I see why it was necessary that the Germans believed ... but the war is over," said Rufus.

Michel turned toward Rufus. "Monsieur Blake, Doctor, my brother and I were born from the same egg, we shared the same genes. I suffered when he suffered. I loved my brother and I love him still. Even when, through my actions, I sentenced him to death, I loved him. I loved him even when I hated him. We still speak to one another, Monsieur, just like we always did when we were children together, without words. I was always part of my brother. Monsieur, when I took on my brother's identity, it was like putting on a jacket I'd worn many times before, a jacket I was already comfortable in. It was easy to become my brother, I am my brother."

Birds for Breakfast

WE DRESSED QUICKLY AND IN SILENCE. That had been the plan, to be up before the rest of the house and away across the dew-licked fields in the early light. We were up early, but we were not the first up. That honour belonged to the village roosters that, for a half-hour past, had been stridently and loudly announcing the new day. Even allowing for the roosters, we were still not first up. The air wafting in through the open windows was suffused with the heady scents of the countryside and the ripe smells of the farmyard. From the kitchen came the pungent aroma of coffee.

Zakis finished dressing first, pulling his belt buckle closed, and slipping into a pair of polished, leather loafers. He chuckled, "In twenty-six years you'd think I might have beaten Papa out of bed just once." Sitting on the narrow cot where I'd spent the night, I finished tying my shoes, then followed Zakis down the shadowed twist of stair.

The main floor of the house was comprised of two rooms: the kitchen living area that we stepped down into and, leading off to one side, a single bedroom, its door closed. This second room was where Zakis' parents slept. There were two other doorways, both usually left open during the day, although now the back door was closed. The front door led out onto a small porch where, under a cone of pale yellow light, Zakis' father Mikis was sitting. Wearing dark, narrow pants and a collarless white shirt buttoned down to the wrists, Mikis was as plain, erect, and angular as the straight-backed chair he sat on. He cradled a small white cup in his lap and, when he turned, the yellow light pooled on his forehead and gave a lurid wash to his creased, leathery features frosted with a day's growth of beard.

"Kalimera agoria, kimithikate kala?"

"Ego kimithika kala, efaristo, Kirio Dysillis," I returned the older man's greeting and assured him that I'd slept well.

Zakis laid his hand on his father's shoulder *"Kala,* Papa, *kala."* We stood silently for a few moments, looking out at the dark, hidden land beyond the small village. The first pale flush of dawn had begun to push back night's shroud and, across the eastern horizon, the dark rumpled outline of the mountains of the Northern Pelopenese loomed out of the retreating dark. A mutter of words passed between the older man and his son. Zakis turned to me, "My father says, he thought we were leaving early and did we realize that the birds we are seeking will be flying, not walking."

Leaving the old man still sitting quietly, we came back inside. Zakis flipped on the light, a 40-watt bulb that only partly brought the room's mix of dusty pewters, smudged shapes and muted patches of colour to life.

"Coffee?" Zakis queried softly, and, without waiting for a reply, took down two small white cups from where they gleamed softly in the box of narrow wooden shelves by the stove. Placing them side-by-side on the scarred wooden counter, he took the lid from a clay pot and shovelled several heaped spoonfuls of coarse brown sugar into the cups. A long-handled copper *briki* was sitting on the stovetop over a tiny flicker of yellow-blue flame. From the bell-shaped pot Zakis filled the cups to the brim with the thick, frothing, chocolate-brown coffee. Over the last year or so I'd become accustomed to the flavour and chewable character of *café turkio*, a taste made palatable only by adding sugar in a ratio of two to one, sugar to coffee. When I'd first come here after two years in Italy, I'd thought *café turkio* a poor substitute for the espressos and cappuccinos I'd become accustomed to in Milan. But the memory of Italian coffee had dwindled and *café turkio*, along with *retsina* and *ouzo*, had become tastes determinedly acquired and fervently defended. I held the cup for a few moments to let the grounds settle and looked out the open door. Soon the sun would climb above the mountains bringing with it the warmth of the day, but now it was still cool, and I let the heat from the cup pulse through my fingers.

Zakis spoke again. "My father says we should leave soon and he is right. The time when the birds pass is short." Zakis paused to take a sip of his coffee. "I have to tell you, Christos, I am looking forward to this morning with great happiness. I am so glad you are here. It is a long time since I went out in the early morning to go shooting with a friend."

A muffled, shuffling announced Zakis' mother who appeared in the darkened doorway that led to her bedroom. She looked to be about the same age as her husband but her skin was pale compared to Mikis' hard and deeply furrowed hide, a result of fifty years of work under an unremitting sun. Zakis' mother wore a long, plain black dress and a knitted black cardigan. Her black hair, seamed with grey, was pulled tightly back from her face, a face that surely had never known joy, a face that took on an even sterner expression as she reproved her son. *"Then boris na pas metipota sto stomahi, yati eisai leptos!"* Saying this, she moved toward the kitchen.

Putting his cup of coffee down on the counter, Zakis stepped to his mother and placed his hands on her shoulders. He leaned down and kissed her frown-wrinkled forehead that came up to his chest and, as I watched, her grim countenance melted away and she smiled almost bashfully. Zakis looked over at me. "My mother will make something for us to take. She worries that you and I will faint from hunger if we go without food for two hours. I think perhaps all mothers are the same?"

I smiled in agreement.

Zakis leaned away from his mother and grinned, but her severe expression returned as she looked at me. *"Pernas oli thi ora na kinigas kopolos touristas. Horis na skeftese tis poutanes!"* Still grinning, Zakis said, "My mother says the same thing whenever she sees me. She thinks Athens is bad for me and that I don't eat enough good food and drink too much. She says we spend too much time chasing tourist girls who have no modesty and are little better than prostitutes." His mother said something else that I didn't catch, and again Zakis translated, "She says that your mother would understand and that boys are a constant headache."

I looked again at Zakis' mother who I decided was not really that old — perhaps in her very early fifties or even late forties. She spoke again to her son. Zakis sighed with mock exasperation. "She says girls are much more useful and don't cause their parents worry." He gave his mother a slight squeeze and then removing his hands from her shoulders said, *"Efaristo,* Mama. Come Christos, you and I will go and get the guns."

Twenty minutes later, the night had drawn further back with only a mass of dark woolly threads remaining in the west. We stepped across the wooden threshold, off the narrow porch, and onto the packed, pale-brown earth that surrounded the house. Zakis had slung a deep leather satchel across his shoulder that contained the food his mother had prepared for us. As we stepped through the door, he turned and spoke to his father who remained expressionless, but nodded and replied. Zakis laughed briefly then said, "I told my father that, when we return, this bag will be stuffed with duck. He said he hopes so and that he has raised a son who is smarter than a duck."

Ersa, the Goddess of Dew, still held the land under her dominion, and the dirt on which we walked didn't cloud around our feet as it would later when the moisture was burned out of it. I was wearing a flap-pocketed, heavy leather jacket that had a musky smell of age and perhaps of the animal whose frame it first graced. Zakis had commented on the jacket only yesterday, when we'd set out from Athens in his small Fiat.

"Christos, where did you get that jacket? It is very Greek, very authentic — leather as thick as rhino hide. But my friend, you smell terrible, like a fox."

I laughed and told him the story of the purchase in detail. "I bought it from a small store in Monastaraki, on that little street by the metro station near that stall that sells *tyropita*." It had not been necessary to tell Zakis it was a used clothing store, only that it was in the old market district of Monastaraki. That was enough; there was no other kind of store in Monastaraki. I remembered the conversation with the owner of the store.

"This jacket, 500 drachmas, that is a lot of money."

"Ah, you are English?" The man had responded, beaming over the counter at me while ignoring the matter of price.

"English, yes," I replied.

"In English my name is George, like your soccer player, Georgie Best." The man's beaming smile almost exceeded the ample limits of his cheeks. "You look like Georgie Best."

"I don't think so"

"I think so," the man named George replied unhesitatingly and with confidence. "Your hair is long like his. What a remarkable coincidence all this is."

"A coincidence?"

"Of course," the man replied, "You look like Georgie Best and my name is George."

"Mmm."

"Five hundred drachmas," George said abruptly, returning to the business at hand. He then repeated the number as though I was missing some generally known truth, "500 drachmas? Of course that is too much, far too much." He'd said this with a theatrically pained expression at having to state something so glaringly obvious. "I am embarrassed that you should think I would attempt to sell at that price, to an Englishman." He shook his head sadly at this Englishman's inability to grasp something so simple. "That price, my friend, is the *American* price," and, still shaking his head added, "Americans are strange people. If the price is too low they will think something is . . . smells fishy. I think that is what the English say, is it not? It is necessary to overcharge Americans so that they will not feel bad, so that they feel they are doing good in the world — like in Vietnam."

"Ah."

"So!" he'd continued expansively, "The *English* price, because it is well-known — if I can say this without giving offence — that the English, unlike the Americans, have no money — the English price is 400 drachmas. This, I think, is a very nice price that you will find most comfortable, I think."

I slipped the jacket on. It fit fairly well, and George purred his approval.

"It looks very good on you, as though made for you. Your woman, she will be very impressed."

I wriggled my shoulders around to get a feel for it. "I have no woman but I agree that it fits fairly well, although it is a little bulky and heavy."

"You prefer boys? In Greece that is very usual, although illegal and if . . . "

"No, no, that's not it." I interjected quickly.

It was bulky, in fact, heavy, but I liked the worn patina and subtle scarring in the thick buttery leather. Certainly it smelled of sheep or maybe goats — although not fox. "I am not a tourist. I live here in Athens and 400 drachmas is more than I can afford. Also, if you don't mind me saying, it has a strange smell, don't you think?"

George listened respectfully, his head lowered as if in deep thought, and looked up only briefly, eyebrow raised, at this last comment.

I ploughed on, "I was really hoping to find something for less, around 250 perhaps," and added ingenuously, "I like the jacket, but perhaps your store is too expensive for me." George's smile disappeared and, for a moment, I thought I'd offended him. Then, like the sun re-emerging from behind a shoulder of passing cloud, the smile re-appeared.

"Ah, now I see you are joking. Two hundred and fifty would be less than I paid for it. But still, you are not a tourist and, of course, that makes a difference, you are almost like one of us, except of course you are English. If you were Greek, you would have known that what you call 'the strange smell' is simply the smell of genuine Greek leather and, without question, it is antique — it has history."

"You speak excellent English," I commented, which was no more than the truth. "Where did you learn?"

George's smile was more of a smirk, almost embarrassed, as though something indecent had passed between us. "I am not from here, I am Greek of course, but Cypriot, from Limasol."

"Ah."

"Had we met only a short time ago, we might have been enemies, I might have had to kill you." George smiled broadly when he said this. "Many English soldiers died on Cyprus. You have heard perhaps of Ledra Street in Nicosia — Murder Mile?"

"Yes, I remember that time, although I was young. I am glad we didn't meet then."

George laughed, "Ah, yes, I thought you were older."

"I was just a teenager then, too young for conscription."

The game with its diversions went on for some minutes more, until, with a price finally agreed upon and it being amicably agreed that the English and the Greeks made better friends than enemies, I left the store 295 drachmas poorer, but wearing the jacket.

Zakis' jacket was also leather, but a very pale leather, almost cream, and probably a third the weight of mine. It was fitted with a belt at the waist, epaulettes at the shoulders, and looked inappropriately new, expensive, effete, and out of place in the country. Like many of his generation of young Greek men with ambition, Zakis had left his village and gone to Athens, first to the University, then stayed on to work after graduation. In Zakis' case this work was at the Bank of Greece. Now he considered himself an Athenian, and no longer simply a villager from the great rural heartland of the country. Eager to differentiate himself from his village origins, he had become a bit of a peacock with a glittering watch, a flashy jacket, and too much cologne. He had looked forward to this weekend in his village, to show how well he had done, to show off his acquisitions, his clothes, his car, his English friend. But now, he'd forgotten all that. He was here as he'd been as a child with his father, a tiny figure in a majestic landscape at the break of day.

Zakis carried his father's over-under, twelve-gauge Beretta cradled in the crook of his elbow, the barrel locked and the shells chambered. I was careful to stay behind him, unhappy at his way of carrying a shotgun. The gun was distinctive: engraved on the receiver and extending along matching side-plates, in gold detail, was a scene of a partridge bursting from cover before a man with a gun. I carried Zakis' quite plain, single-barrel Benelli, the breach broken and gaping open the way I'd been taught many years ago by my grandfather on his small farm in Yorkshire. That was before the horror of myxomatosis, when there were still wild rabbits to shoot, a time when rabbits ran rampant and bred faster than they could be reduced by any number of eleven-year-old boys with .410 shotguns.

The village was quiet, with nobody about, although the occasional noise from inside a house or a dimly lit window gave proof that, Easter or not, the routine and imperatives of rural life went on. Very quickly, the scatter of white and ochre houses petered out, and the dirt track snaked away through the fields to join the coast road that lay a handful of miles distant. That road ran along the Gulf of Corinth, across the startling, arrow-straight canal that bisected the Isthmus of Corinth as though a giant maul had cleaved the earth, and from there, back to Athens. It was the way we had come yesterday to spend Easter with Zakis and his family.

Once out of the village, we stepped off the dirt road and set off across the ragged, tufted grassland. In the west, the last of the night fog had lifted although batons of mist still lay trapped in the hollows of the land waiting to be released by the coming warmth of the day, a day now heralded by a thin golden line stitched along the crest of the mountains edging the Gulf.

Crossing the flank of a hillside, we paused and looked back to where the low-lying village had merged into the blue landscape and teal shadows. We plodded silently onwards, with only the sound of the wet grasses rushing against our clothes, and the occasional soft grunt accompanying our excertions.

Breaking a silence of several minutes, Zakis said abruptly, "I wish we could have come earlier — sooner? Which is more correct, Christos? "

"They are the same; it makes no difference."

"Ah. Last week my uncles went boar hunting. That would have been very exciting and different for you. Do you ride, Christos? Also, I think now all the birds are gone to Africa. Have you ever hunted boar Christos?"

I said I'd ridden, but hadn't hunted boar. "In England there are no wild boar and, anyway, hunting is something for the upper classes."

Zakis considered this carefully before replying. "I don't think that can be true, Christos. Hunting is a countryman's love. Every countryman hunts."

I thought about that. "Maybe you're right, maybe I was just thinking of our aristocracy. 'The unspeakable in pursuit of the uneatable' is how they have been described."

Zakis paused, then said, "I am not sure I understand. What does unspeakable mean?"

"Something that can barely be described in words," I replied.

Again pausing, Zakis said, "The boar is very exciting. He is fierce and dangerous, quite without fear, but of course he does not want to be killed."

"I imagine not."

"I think you would say he is, 'tough as old boots'? I have heard that."

"It is an expression," I replied.

"Like your jacket perhaps?"

"It is true that it could be more supple," I said, "and lighter."

We had seen a few big birds flying high, too high to waste optimism and shotgun shells on. We had walked for about half an hour when Zakis stopped and pointed to a fallen tree.

"Christos, let us sit here and wait. Soon something must come within range. We have lots of time and we can eat while we wait." He rested his shotgun against the trunk and sat down.

I followed suit and, because it was getting warm, thought about taking the heavy jacket off, but decided against it. The morning was hardly born, maybe half an hour or so longer before the real warmth came, and it would be cumbersome to carry. We drank from the flasks of water each of us had brought with us. After wiping my mouth with the back of my hand, I pushed the cork into the top of the leather flask and said, "It's surprising how cool the water keeps in these."

Zakis grunted then said, "So, Chris, this is where I was born and lived all my childhood; she is beautiful do you think?" As he spoke, he opened the satchel, and the sudden explosion of smells — fresh bread, rosemary, ham, and cheese — wafted before my nose. I took the crust of bread, a slab of rosemary-cured ham, and the slice of pine-coloured local cheese that Zakis held out. My mouth began to water. I didn't answer Zakis' question, but tore into the food like a starving man. We sat in silence, mouths full, grinning like idiots at each other.

"God bless your mother, Zakis," I said.

"Yes. God bless my mother," replied Zakis.

We were still preoccupied with eating when, flashing colour and calling out, a flight of ducks clattered by no higher than the treetops. Zakis uttered an oath, dropped his food, grabbed his gun, and brought it to his shoulder. But the ducks were gone, their chatter faded, and Zakis' food lay scattered among the grass and rocks. Zakis stooped to retrieve a piece of the cheese, dusted if off, and popped it in his mouth. He looked over. "There will be more, Christos." I nodded, but was glad the ducks had got away, wild and alive in their flight.

As the sun climbed higher, we got warmer, but the only things flying were insects. Some bigger birds flew by but high up out of reach.

"Your father's gun is beautiful, Zakis. The engraving is elegant and finely detailed."

"That is true, Christos. Are you perhaps wondering how does a simple Greek farmer who lives in such a village in the Peloponnese have such a weapon?"

"I hadn't quite thought that far but, as you mention it, it is the kind of gun I would expect to see on an English estate."

"Christos, this country was occupied by Hitler's ally, Mussolini. There were many Italian soldiers here until Italy collapsed and the Germans came. Perhaps the Italian officers thought the Greeks would offer no resistance, that it would be pleasant to spend time hunting, and so brought their shotguns with them. My father has never said how he came by it, but I know it came from the war and I don't think it was a gift."

"Ah," I said.

We watched the day unfold further.

"The sky is completely empty," Zakis complained. "I think that those ducks were the only ones in the whole Pelopenese."

"Maybe," I agreed. "It seems now that the word is out and that they are avoiding us."

Another half-hour passed and we talked more about the guns and the different kinds of birds in the area. "The Benelli that you have was my first gun — my father got it for me when I was ten. It is a very good gun, but of course it has only one barrel." Zakis reached over and picked up the Benelli. "This was one of the first shotguns that Benelli made." He snapped the breach closed, lifted the shotgun to his shoulder, and swung it in an arc across the sky. "Before making shotguns, they made motorcycles, and their bikes won many races before the war, even your Isle of Man T.T. race." Zakis lowered the weapon, snapped open the breech and returned it to where it had rested. "You are correct to carry your weapon like that. I should do the same, but I am always careful."

I told Zakis about shooting rabbit when I was young and how, after myxomatosis was introduced, that was pretty much the end of wild rabbits. Zakis nodded, "We had it here too, although before my time. We still have rabbit, but not so many. I prefer to shoot birds, though. Turtledoves are very good, but they are not as many now as there used to be."

"Maybe too many are being shot?" I suggested.

Zakis scoffed at the idea. "No, Christos. There are many turtledoves and the few that we shoot will make no difference. It is those that use nets that make a difference."

Finally succumbing to the increasing warmth, Zakis took off his jacket, and after brushing a few grains of dirt from the log laid the jacket carefully across it. He looked up at the sky, which was devoid of life unless you counted the condensation trail of a jet tracking inch by inch across the firmament. "I am sorry, Christos, this is not good." We waited some more, talked some more, searched the heavens some more, and then fell silent.

Abruptly, Zakis got to his feet. He slung his jacket and satchel across his shoulder and picked up the Beretta. "Come, Christos. What we are going to do is not what you English would call sporting, but we cannot go back empty-handed." I picked up the Benelli and followed Zakis through the shrub.

"See the tree, Christos?" Zakis said, pointing away to the east. And indeed it was impossible not to see the tree, a solitary, spreading giant standing a half-mile distant.

"I see it," I answered.

"You cannot tell from here, but it is a spot where many small birds come to roost, *helidoni*, we call them in Greek. I think you call them sparrows perhaps?" Zakis said this somewhat apologetically. "My mother will scald them and remove all the feathers and, how do you say, the insides?"

"Innards," I corrected. "It means the same, just a different way of . . . in this context, a better way . . . "

"Yes, innards, she will take those out of course. The rest we will eat. They are very tasty with eggs, for breakfast, like the English breakfast, bacon and eggs."

"You eat the whole bird?" I asked.

"Of course, it is very good, you will see."

"The head?"

"You will see."

With the tree now only a couple of hundred yards off, the land fell away somewhat toward a narrow stream — perhaps a dozen feet across — that wound its way sluggishly through the unkempt meadow.

"Christos, after we cross we will take different directions. This way, if the birds should fly away before we get close, one of us may have a chance. If we get all the way to the tree and they are still there, I will count to three and then we will fire."

"You are right, Zakis; it is not very sporting," I said, but was already hungry again and the prospect of bacon and eggs or something like it was appealing. In two steps, I was down the shallow bank and into the stream, picking my way quickly across, slipping a couple of times on the mossy, smooth, round stones, and taking water into my running shoes. I squelched out the other side and, turning back, saw Zakis looking down uncertainly at his leather loafers. I laughed, "It's only water, Zakis."

"It's my own fault, Christos. I should not have worn these. They are good for Athens, not so good for the Pelopenese, and they were not cheap." Zakis looked at the stream and the precarious shining slivers of rock he would need to skip across on if he was to avoid going ankle deep in the water as I had. He had been, I thought, far too long in the city. Zakis stepped carefully down the bank, that was barely a bank at all, toward the water. Feeling it was unbecoming to await the opportunity to gloat, I turned back through the bright tall grass and up the shallow rise away from the stream. Looking toward the tree, I could see at least a score or so of small birds roosting.

There was nothing to separate the sudden blast and the giant hand that smashed me violently forward and flat on my face in the grass. The Benelli flew from my grip and I lay stunned and uncomprehending on the ground.

There was a long moment of absolute silence and then I heard Zakis yelling and splashing in the stream. "Christos! Christos!" It took me only moments to begin to realize what must have happened. I wondered how badly I'd been injured and if the lack of sensation was a prelude to dying. Then Zakis was next to me, his English forgotten, babbling in Greek, my name being the only word I understood.

I felt a crawling, craven fear in my entrails as I contemplated the extent of damage a double-barrel twelve gauge would have caused, "Is there much blood, Zakis?" I asked fearfully. I could hear the panic in Zakis' voice and knew it must be bad.

"Can you move your arms at all, Christos? I want to see . . . can you move them down?"

I sent a timorous message to my fingers to move, and from the corner of my eye, saw them respond. I moved my arms gingerly down from the crucified position I'd been sent sprawling into. I felt Zakis ease my jacket from my shoulders. There was a long silence and I lay unmoving. I didn't even try to move, lest I make matters worse.

"My God," said Zakis.

I felt the panic rise. Who would tell my parents? They barely knew what country I was in. Had I even written them since I left Milan? What about my plans for university next year? And sex? I probably hadn't had sex more than a dozen times. I was too young, too young to die in a field in Greece. "Zakis." I said, "How bad is it?"

"Christos, my friend, I don't believe this but, there's no injury."

"What do you mean no injury, Zakis? You bloody shot me!"

"Christos, this jacket of yours, nothing went through."

"What do you mean, nothing went through?"

"I mean, Christos, this jacket, it's like armour-plate; there's not a mark on you," replied Zakis. "Your jacket's destroyed, but no shot went through."

I considered Zaki's comments carefully for a moment until, disbelieving, I rolled carefully onto my side. Moving very slowly, I pushed myself up onto my hands and knees. It was true that I felt no searing pain, nothing worse than a stinging across my buttocks, and my back ached like I'd been hit hard with something heavy. Resting on one arm, I used the other hand to awkwardly explore the area around my kidneys, to probe further up my spine and between my shoulder blades. I felt no wet patch, and no shredded shirt.

"You see?" said Zakis.

"I'm okay," I confirmed, somewhat awed.

Zakis held up my jacket with the inside toward me. The nylon lining was unmarked. Then he turned it around. Hundreds of tiny tears and eruptions covered almost the entire back. I looked at Zakis and shook my head. "As tough as old boots."

The birds had flown after that first shotgun blast, and we had to wait a while for their return. A half-hour later we approached the tree carefully, without talking. Zakis was carrying the Beretta over his shoulder, although now the breach was open. As we came close, a couple of the birds lifted out of the branches and flew off. Zakis held up his hand and we stopped. I eased the breach closed on the Benelli. Zakis, likewise, locked the Beretta before calling across in an exaggerated whisper, "I will count to three." We pointed our guns up into the branches. "Now!" said Zakis. I squeezed the trigger.

For the second time that morning, shotgun blasts shattered the early quiet. A thin drift of smoke stood for a moment in the still, cordite-scented air. Among a small shower of twigs and leaves, perhaps eight or nine birds fluttered or dropped to the grass. Some were dead, some peeping piteously. Zakis moved quickly, joyously and, without differentiating the living from the dead, plucked the tiny bodies from the ground and stuffed them into his bag. The sun was now well up, and the landscape sparkled with light and life. We strode off purposefully toward the village, full of our manhood, our hunters' pathetic bombast. I carried the ruined jacket over my shoulder, the jacket I would never wear again. Breakfast was the best I'd ever eaten. Days afterwards, I was still finding twelve-gauge pellets in my pant cuffs.

The Watch Seller

"HEY, ENGLISH BOY!" THE VOICE LISPED from behind me, from over my right shoulder. It was Christmas of '69, December 19 to be exact, and the sky over Athens was a clear shiny blue, as blue as in a child's painting, with not a wisp of cloud anywhere. The temperature, even at nine in the morning, was shirtsleeve balmy, quite unlike the circumstances of my life, which were, in fact, quite bleak.

Sitting atop an outcrop of veined, white rock across from the Parthenon, the shine of the ocean an hour distant, I was looking toward that other high point of Athens, Lykavittos, sharp and clear in the morning light. Below me lay the old district of Plaka with its narrow, twisting and steeply stepped streets, an innately exotic place that, for the last year, I'd called home. Among the hodgepodge of pink-tiled roofs, white walls, and tiny rooftop gardens, part of the rooftop patio of my rented apartment was just visible. At the corner of the patio was a stunted orange tree with fruit as bitter as the knowledge that the income from the last English lesson I'd given two weeks earlier was all but gone. I had no part of the rent due in two weeks, and certainly neither the means, nor the inclination to celebrate the festive season. In fact, all that stood between me and abject destitution were a couple of hundred drachmas. It was this knowledge that prevented me from snapping out, *Ohi*, beat it. Instead I looked around.

Like two thirds of the male population of Greece, the man wore a heavy black moustache and a day's growth of beard. A hirsute type accessorized with reflector sunglasses, an affectation shared most notably with the police and security services. Older than me, perhaps by five years, it was hard to say. He was also a couple of inches shorter and ten pounds heavier. Under an ill-fitting, long, blue suit jacket, he wore a plain white shirt open at the neck, through which, as though making its escape, a dark shrub of hair thrust upward and outward, a flash of gold caught within its foliage. Completing this intriguing ensemble, light brown, flared pants settled over the tops of pointed-toed shoes that stuck out like a pair of black beetles.

"You want to make some money, English boy?" he asked.

"Who doesn't?" I replied.

Emboldened, the man moved closer and perched on a piece of roughly worked marble, cast-off presumably by the masons that three thousand years before had worked to create the perfect structure that lay behind us, the temple of Athena, the Parthenon.

"That is surely a fact, we all need money," he responded. Then, holding out his hand, "My name is Kostas, Kostas Grievas."

"Nick," I replied, reaching over to take his hand, which was as damp as I suspected it might be.

"In Greek, that would be Nikos," said Kostas.

"*Thelo* Nick"

"*Ah! Katalavenes Helenki?*"

"*Ohi,* only a little, I have lived here for a year," I answered.

"Yes, I recognize you," said Kostas, nodding his head, "I've seen you here before. I am a frequent visitor myself. Do you live close by?"

I nodded toward Plaka, "Down the hill, Lisiu Street."

"Ah," said Kostas, removing from the pocket of his jacket a large yellow handkerchief with which he began to dab at the warts of perspiration popping out from under his hairline.

I didn't reply and we sat in silence for a moment.

"How is it in Lisiu Street, Nikos?" Kostas asked

"It's Nick and it's noisy. There's a *taverna* or *bquat* on every corner, but the place I have, I don't pay that much, it's very small," I said, resisting the faint impulse to point it out.

"Still," said Kostas, "it is the best part of Athens. It is the heart of Athens, the old town."

"Yes," I agreed. "I lived for a while in Kypseli, but here it is better, not as comfortable, but better."

"Ah, yes," said Kostas.

Once again, we lapsed into a silence, and I thought it best to get back to the point of our conversation, "So, Kostas, you mentioned money I believe?"

Kostas leaned forward and, with the finesse of a magician, returned the handkerchief to the right-hand pocket of his jacket while producing, with a flourish from his left, two shot glasses and a hip flask.

"A present from an American friend," he said by way of explanation, and then, "Metaxas." Kostas poured the viscous gold liquid into the two glasses he held cupped in his left hand. "So, Nikos, how do you make your living, my friend?"

I took the proffered glass and looked across at him. His eyes were invisible behind the mirror glass in which I could see, darkly, only fragments of sky, and of myself. "I teach," I replied guardedly. There were two possibilities to consider. The first, that this man Kostas Grievas was a homosexual and this was a come-on. It would not have been the first time, with previous encounters including a flagrantly open fly as an enticement. However, there was really nothing about Kostas' manner that suggested this motive. The second possibility was a rather more sinister one. I'd been there more than a year and my three-month tourist visa had long ago expired. Possibly my new "friend" was some sort of government immigration agent? No. That didn't seem likely. A greater, and more alarming possibility was that he was Secret Police. My students, typically, were politically of the left and opposed to the American-backed, right-wing government of Papadopoulos, not to mention the war then raging in Vietnam. It was dangerous to be overtly opposed to either; to be so made you a target for abduction or worse. Not for me. I held a British passport.

For my students it was different. One of these, an outspoken member of the students' union, had been taken by the police for questioning a couple of months earlier and had not been seen since. The activities of the pervasive darker elements of the government security services were more than just cause for paranoia — they were cause for caution. But this man, Secret Police? The term was something of a misnomer. Far from secret, they tended to be of a recognizable type — young, vain and beautifully groomed — and while it was true that, like Kostas, they wore reflector sunglasses, they wore *designer* reflector sunglasses. Not even for the sake of an arrest would they wear cheap knock-offs like the ones in which I was seeing my reflection, nor would they dress as garishly as Kostas, or hang out at a tourist trap like the

Parthenon. Routinely, these not so shadowy government agents would be found languishing at the Museu Gardens, or at some of the more stylish coffee houses off Constitution Square. There was little possibility of identifying subversives at these venues, but every possibility of scoring one of the young, or not-so-young, tourist women, so long as they were blonde. American women were preferred; English and German girls in their tiny mini-skirts and skimpy tops were regarded as little better than prostitutes. So, I decided Kostas was the genuine article; his hustler appearance and approach carried the undeniable stamp of authenticity. I just didn't know yet what his hustle was.

"Ah! You teach. At a school of English?" Kostas asked with deliberate ingenuousness.

I ignored the question, but he'd guessed correctly that I was not at a school but making money from private lessons, and that, almost certainly, I had no work permit, which was true. No work permit, no taxes, and no guarantee of quality, a good thing because that was not what I was providing.

When I'd arrived in Athens with twenty pounds sterling in my pocket, my first action was to find out the name of the English language newspaper, *The Athens News*, as it transpired. The small ad that I placed in it read, "English gentleman resident in Athens, offers English language instruction at your home, 100 drachmas an hour." Aside from England being my place of birth, my sole qualification for teaching English was an 'O' level in the subject. I had passed, indeed had taken, only two 'O' levels, the other being Art. The 'A' levels required for university admission had quite exceeded both my reach and my ambition. Fortunately for me, the old adage about the regal qualities conferred upon the one-eyed man in the kingdom of the blind is as true of language as it is of sight. I enjoyed regal status in a city where, to get on in an increasingly international business environment, a command of English was more than desirable; it was essential.

Never having taught a day's English in my life, the one absolute requirement I asked of my students was that they already possess a very good grasp of it. The lessons, if what I was doing could be dignified with such a term, were usually a reading from *Goldfinger* or *Casino Royale*, or whatever I could find in the used section of the English language bookstore off Syntagma Square. As well, lessons were most often arranged by me to coincide with the typical lunch or supper time at the student's home. The justification for such timing was the importance of using English in typical social interactions — for example, meal times. Expressions such as, "Are you hungry?", "Do you want more wine?", "May I offer you a cigarette?" and, to encourage the use of idiom, "It's raining cats and dogs," were exhaustively critiqued and refined. The net result of this tuition strategy was twofold. After several such lessons, I was routinely greeted at the start of a lesson with "Good afternoon, Professor Nick, help yourself to a cigarette. Would you care for a drop of wine?" To which my reply, depending on mood and the time of day, would be, "Yes, thank you, Zakis, Maria, etcetera." Or, "It is rather warm today. Would a cold Amstel be possible?" The opportunity for using "it's raining cats and dogs" seldom presented itself. The second, although unintended, outcome was that a previously abstemious and promising young member of Athens' professional class would have developed an alcohol dependency.

"Yes I teach," I reaffirmed, somewhat coldly. Although, at least in my mind, I had eliminated the two most unpromising prospects, the fact of the matter was that I was interested in making money, at that moment, very interested. My not overly strenuous working schedule of about six hours of a week over the past year had provided enough income for all of my immediate financial needs. But it left no surplus to set aside for occasions like Christmas, when Athens drained like a sink, a good part of its population returning to villages in the Peloponnese and elsewhere to spend time with their families. No students, no lessons, no money.

"You asked me if I was interested in making money," I asked abruptly, keen to leave the question of my employment behind.

"Ah, you are right, I was digressing," admitted Kostas, "and I see that you *are* . . . interested in making money, that is. Perhaps your profession is not in so much demand over Christmas?"

Had he read my mind?

Kostas began to remove from his wrist a chunky watch with the name Seiko clearly engraved across the face. "As you can see, this is a very expensive watch and cost me a lot of money," he said.

"Go on," I said, wondering how this man could afford a watch worth three to four-thousand drachmas.

Kostas opened his jacket a little further and I could see that there were a half-dozen similar, indeed identical, watches pinned to the inside of his coat. He looked at me and smiled. "Of course they are not Seikos, but they are very good copies, even down to the name. And who is to know, maybe they are every bit as superbly excellent?"

I resisted the impulse to comment on his inappropriate combination of superlatives, "All right," I said, "you have me interested. You want me to sell your watches for you. But why would you not sell them yourself?"

Kostas sighed and, sitting erect, lowered his arms to either side of his torso, the palms of his hands open in the unmistakable gesture of complete candour. "Nikos, look at me, I am a simple, poor Greek who could never afford a genuine Seiko." Before continuing, he scratched his belly thoughtfully, at what I imagined was the bearskin rug of hair that covered it. "You however, are a good-looking young Englishman whose loving father bought him a Seiko at great cost for his twenty-first birthday. Sadly, your beautiful young English girlfriend, blonde of course . . . , " Kostas paused for a moment to peer at me hopefully, "perhaps you have such a girlfriend? Maybe a photograph?" I confessed I had neither. "No matter," and Kostas pulled from his pocket a small picture of a beautiful young girl with shining blonde hair, clearly cut from a magazine, and handed it across to me. "Your beautiful young girlfriend," he repeated. "You have just heard she has become very sick in . . . Amsterdam . . . yes, Amsterdam, even as she was coming out to join you here, perhaps to marry? Perhaps she is pregnant? I don't know, Nikos, I will leave the details to you."

"I see," I said, holding the photograph and looking at the picture of the girl. "So, I need the money to travel to Amsterdam. Why should she not go to her parents, they are closer? And this photograph, no one is going to believe that a picture clearly torn from a magazine is my girlfriend. I mean really, no one is going to fall for this."

Kostas looked at me with undisguised disappointment. "It is true what they say of the English, they have no imagination." He shook his head sadly. "Nikos, listen to me, I know Greeks. They love a story. They love a story almost as much as they love a deal. It is because they love a deal more, that they will accept the story." Kostas manoeuvred the Seiko back onto his wrist and then, the watch in place, leaned forward, "Nikos, to tell a good story you have to first believe it yourself, yes? If you don't believe it, how will others? You are a good-looking young man, a proud, educated Englishman, a Professor of English, in fact. Why would you not have a beautiful young girlfriend like the girl in the picture? And why would it not be from a magazine? She is a model. Why would she not have a picture in a magazine? Maybe she was on assignment in Amsterdam. She is probably Swedish, don't you think, with hair like that?" Kostas held out his hand for the picture, and I returned it to him. He studied it for a moment. "We Greeks are crazy for girls like this, not dark and hairy like our own women. Anyway, what about her parents? They are dead, tragically, or perhaps she is, what is the word, estranged? She is your woman, you are destroyed by worry for her, you want only to fly to her . . . " Again Kostas paused. "My God! I should have been a poet. Do you not find this story moving?" I looked across at him to see if he was serious. Kostas smiled. "You English have ice in your veins," he said.

"No one is going to believe such a story, Kostas," I repeated.

Kostas shook his head. "I promise you, Nikos, if I believe the story even as I am inventing it, how will not the foolish greedy Greeks hoping to profit from your tragedy?"

"You seem to have little respect for your countrymen," I said.

"To tell the truth, I am more Turkish than Greek, but I have been here a long time, perhaps now I am more Greek than Turkish. But, ah, whatever I am, I know my countrymen well. And anyway, in any country, money is money."

A tourist coach, air brakes hissing, ground to a stop behind us. With another hiss the door slid open and a throng of camera-festooned Japanese tourists were disgorged out onto the sandy roadway. Within moments cameras were clicking and whirring, and it seemed entirely possible that, for many, their only view of this majestic memory of ancient Athens, would be framed through the viewfinder of a 35mm SLR.

Kostas had removed the watch from his wrist and was holding it loosely. I reached over, and he relinquished it easily. The watch was heavy and certainly didn't look in any way cheap. It looked and felt like quality. I looked up at Kostas, "I can't just go to someone on the street."

"Put the watch on. Trust me, and you and I will make money this afternoon." Sitting up straight, Kostas placed his hands on his knees. "For every watch you sell, you will make three-hundred drachmas — if you sell the watch for fifteen hundred drachmas. If you sell the watch for more than fifteen hundred, we will split the additional profit fifty-fifty." Pushing his hands down on his knees, Kostas got to his feet. "Come, we will take a walk into town and make some money."

I guess I was an easy mark. I was desperate. We walked down from the Parthenon through Plaka and the market district of Monastaraki. At this time of day, there was no live music, only taped, but the familiar and distinctive sound of *bazouki* threaded the air, as did the smell of grilling meat and herbs. We stopped at a small stall selling *tyropita*, and Kostas bought us one each.

"We will go to the area behind Constitution, that is where we will find those with money and with egos to feed, those who know what a Seiko is, who want to own one, but have not quite so much money as they think they deserve. They will go for our story because they see an opportunity to buy class at bargain prices. Of course, you cannot buy class at any price, but you can buy its appearance, and that is all that they can hope for."

I looked at Kostas with new respect and thought that perhaps he should be teaching psychology, and not selling watches on the streets of Athens.

"So English boy, with your beautiful, sick, blonde girlfriend, here is some money; go into this café. It is a popular place for lunch with people from the banks and offices in this area. Sit out on the patio at a table next to the street; hold the watch in your hands and think of your story," said Kostas.

I did as I was instructed, took a table by the window overlooking the sidewalk, and ordered ouzo from the gangly waiter in a white jacket who stooped like an egret at my elbow. I took off the 'Seiko' and laid it on the table in front of me. I decided on my story. My girlfriend was pregnant and had gone into labour six weeks early. She was in Amsterdam, visiting her sick mother; she was estranged from her father. She . . . I couldn't go on. It was ridiculous. There was no way I was going to make this believable. I took out the picture and looked at it again. I should be so lucky. The music was typical *bazouki*-backed folk music about some young men and their passion for a local girl. Not long ago it might have been the music of Theodarakis but, because of his left-wing views, he was never played in public now, only behind closed doors with the volume down low. I looked around at my fellow diners. It was early and the place was half-empty. Not a place for tourists; I was the only non-Greek. The waiter appeared with my ouzo and a small plate of *mezes*. Kostas' money would be paying for this and, however small the cost, I decided I owed him one try. I finished the small plate of feta cheese, olives, tomato, *octopithi*, and of course the ouzo. I caught the eye of the waiter and signalled for another.

I looked around again. There were more people now, busy eating and talking. I could not imagine how to start. The waiter reappeared with my second ouzo, a small jug of water, and another plate of *mezes*, the small token hors d'oeuvres that always accompany a glass. I poured the water into the ouzo and watched the familiar milkiness cloud the clear liquor. Already I could feel the slight numbness caused by the alcohol and was reminded that I had inherited my father's weak head for it. I looked around once more — mostly couples, some clearly business, some more obviously romantic. What was I supposed to do, just go up to some complete stranger's table, interrupt the conversation and ask, in a language they probably wouldn't understand, if they wanted to buy my watch?

While I was contemplating this dilemma, Kostas appeared. Ignoring me completely, he took a seat at the table next to mine. He ordered a glass of *domestica* and a plate of *dolmathas*, then opened the daily newspaper and sat back in his chair. A few minutes later, mellowed by my second ouzo, but no further ahead in implementing our sales strategy, I was startled when Kostas abruptly leaned over and, in a voice loud enough to be heard several tables away, addressed me in Greek. I understood little of what he said, although it was clear by his gestures and by the word Seiko popping up a couple of times that he was commenting on my watch, which still lay on the table in front of me. I replied in Greek that I was English and did not speak Greek, for which I apologized.

"Oh sir, please," said Kostas, switching to English, "no apologies are necessary. I said simply that, that is a magnificent watch, a Seiko I believe, and a model I have not seen until now although, of course, I have seen pictures in magazines. You are very fortunate, sir, to have such a watch; it must have cost a small fortune, even in pounds?" Kostas spoke with such sincerity and seemingly unfeigned enthusiasm that I began myself to believe that the watch was something special. As well, I had become aware as Kostas was speaking, of a couple of heads turning in our direction. I took advantage of the lead Kostas had given me and launched into our roughly sketched-out story. The watch was a twenty-first birthday present. I didn't feel ready for fatherhood so my girlfriend was no longer pregnant, just sick, and I was in need of airfare to Amsterdam. I even overcame my reluctance and pulled out the ludicrous magazine photograph that Kostas had given me, that he now exclaimed over, taking it carefully from me to share with the man at the table next to him. He also showed it to our waiter, who had been hovering in the wings, and to a second waiter who, despite being encumbered with an armful of empty plates, had allowed his curiosity to get the better of him and wandered over. I caught the English word 'model' amidst Kostas' repeated explanation of my supposed plight, the tragic dimensions of which, judging by their faces, was no doubt amplified by my girlfriend's beauty.

Kostas was all compassion, "Ah, I am so sorry, my friend, to have to part with such a treasure, a gift from your departed father as well . . . but for such a girl, such a girl." Kostas took on a mien of tragic shadings that would not have looked out of place in an opera, perhaps a comic opera. I felt he must be overdoing it. How could anyone believe our little tale?

After repeating to the assembly in Greek what he had just said to me in English, Kostas turned back toward me. "My name is Kostas, and yours?" I guess we had to make the pretence that we had not previously met, so I told him and he continued, "Forgive me for asking, Nikos, but my friend here, Yanis," Kostas indicated with a nod to our waiter, who stood at his shoulder, "wishes to know if your girlfriend is naturally blonde?"

I looked with astonishment at Kostas, who looked back at me with unblinking gravity and said, in a voice heavy with meaning, "I think she must be, yes?"

"Yes, of course she is; she's naturally blonde, of course." And then warming to the idiocy of it all, I assured Kostas that the picture did not show her well, and that in life she was much more blonde than the photograph suggested.

Kostas repeated what I had said to the small group, including now, a second customer who had come over and was rewarded with a circle of approving nods and murmurs. Retrieving the picture, Kostas gazed at it soulfully once more before returning it to me, and I, in my turn, tucked it reverentially back into my wallet.

Kostas shook his head sadly. "I only wish I had the seventeen-hundred drachmas myself, just to help you, you understand, although I would feel a thief to pay so little." Kostas paused before adding firmly, "But, that you say is the cost of your ticket." He then turned to our audience to whom, I presumed, he repeated his musings in Greek.

The man eating alone at the next table, whose interest had been piqued either by the watch or the picture of my supposed girlfriend — it was by now difficult to say which was generating more interest — said something in Greek I didn't understand. Kostas replied rapidly and at length, and I again caught the words 'model' and 'airplane'.

"May I?" asked Kostas with impressive humility as he picked up the watch and handed it to the man. The latter was a businessman of some sort. He wore a dark suit and tie, and had the look of a professional, or perhaps a government worker of which there were many in Athens. Taking the watch from Kostas, he turned it over a couple of times and then held it to his ear. He looked across at me and said in heavily accented and halting English, "I am sorry for your trouble. Your girlfriend is very beautiful, but I have a watch."

"Thank you, of course," I replied, my expression suitably grave.

"May I?"

I looked up. The waiter, Yanis, leaned in, now even more like an egret spotting its prey, and picked up the watch. "I know watches," he said. I felt a prickle of alarm and Kostas' grin assumed a strangely fixed appearance. Like the man at the next table, Yanis turned the watch over a few times and held it to his ear. He shook it gently, held it to his ear again, then examined the back. He handed the watch back to me. "This watch . . ." he said. I held my breath and realized that my palms were sweating, " . . . how much will you take for it? What is your best price?"

I breathed again and Kostas' smile took on a less maniacal glare. "Well, I'm hoping for seventeen hundred drachmas," I said, "I know it's worth more, but I need the money right away so . . . I suppose I would take . . . "

"I will give you fifteen hundred, " said Kostas, "it is more than I can afford, but when again in my life will I ever have the chance to own a watch like this, and for only a fraction of its real worth? If we are agreed I will go now to my bank and I will need to make some arrangements and . . . "

"I will pay you sixteen hundred," said the waiter. "I will pay you cash, and I will pay you now," he added, reaching into his back pocket and pulling out a worn leather wallet.

Kostas tried his best to look crestfallen.

I looked at the watch that I was holding in my hand and did my equal best to look conflicted. "I don't know . . . I . . . do you think, do you believe my father would understand?" I asked softly. Kostas reached over and put his hand on my shoulder and with a show of reluctance at what was clearly a painful parting, I held out the watch to the waiter.

Coming to his feet, Kostas transferred his hand from my shoulder to the waiter's arm and speaking in Greek said what I later learned was, "You have done a good thing for this young man and his girlfriend. And if you have also gained a small treasure, then that is only just. I would gladly have paid more. It is surely worth more but, like any married man, I am not entirely the master of my life. To buy such a luxury, even at such a price would have caused problems at home. Such a work of art, a watch you will be proud to one day hand down to your son."

With a faint shrug and just the suggestion of a smile, the waiter laid the sixteen hundred drachmas on the table, took the watch and, shooting back his sleeve, fastened it onto his wrist. He then extended his arm, angling his wrist to better enjoy the full splendour of his new acquisition, and was joined in this admiration by the small assembly. Kostas, misty eyed, looked on with feigned envy, before leaving the price of his lunch on the table and slipping from the restaurant.

Pride of ownership satisfied, the waiter, his watch arm extended somewhat before him and having declined my attempts to pay the bill, returned to the kitchen. I slipped the sixteen one-hundred drachma notes into the pocket of my jeans and headed out into the street. Standing across the way, Kostas, once he was certain I'd seen him, turned and began to walk.

"So, Nikos what do you think, was that easy money or not? Did I not say that we would make money this afternoon? Seven drachmas on ouzo, twenty minutes work, and you are three hundred and fifty drachmas better off than when we met at the Parthenon this morning." Kostas sat back smiling. We were now at a little café, not far from the place where we had made our first score. Kostas, in an expansive mood had ordered *yuvarelakia* and a bottle of *retsina* for us and paid me what he had promised. I felt obliged to tell him that Yanis, the proud new owner of the watch, had refused to let me pay for my drinks, but Kostas waved away my attempt to repay him the ten drachmas, "You and I will make so much money Nikos, what is ten drachmas between partners?"

"Kostas, you were right, but I have to say I feel uneasy about this. It doesn't seem right, do you understand?"

Kostas frowned. "Nikos, what is it that you feel uneasy about, my friend? You speak as if we have done something wrong." Kostas speared a meatball and, waving it from side to side, outlined his moral position. "Nikos, did you see the joy on that man's face when he put his new watch on, his pride? What can you feel bad about that you made someone happy? Is this some other strange English thing, that happiness is bad?" He popped the meatball in his mouth, shrugged his shoulders, and raised his eyebrows.

I didn't want to seem ungrateful, I had just made three-hundred and fifty drachma, but my conscience compelled me to raise the matter of the watches' provenance. "Kostas, the watches are not Seikos, or at least you tell me they're not. Are they stolen? If not, where are they from that we can make this profit?"

Kostas continued to deconstruct the meatball, announcing the completion of the process with a sip of wine and a small belch. He looked me in the eye, "Nikos, you offend me. I am a businessman not a thief. I ... "

"I'm sorry, Kostas, I didn't ... "

Kostas held up his hand, his fork pointing at the ceiling. "It doesn't matter, Nikos . . . you don't know me, we met this morning. You have no reason to trust me, although I had hoped . . . "

"Kostas, I . . . "

"Let me finish, Nikos. I am as I say, a businessman, as you are — an entrepreneur. I don't know, perhaps your profession, a professor of English, is more exalted, more ethical . . . ." He paused, looked at me, and must surely have seen me wince before continuing. "I speak five languages. Do you not think I could teach English as well as you? Perhaps better because I also speak Greek?" Kostas looked at me waiting for my reply. I stayed silent and Kostas smiled.

"My name is not Kostas. My name is Atwar, I am Turkish. I speak Turkish, Greek, German, Italian, and, of course, English. If I was known as Turkish here, life would be more difficult. So, Kostas — the most common Greek name."

"Kostas, I'm sorry. I didn't mean to suggest . . . "

"But you did suggest, Nikos. You suggested at least the possibility that they were stolen. No?"

"I did, and I'm sorry. I . . . "

"Let me tell you, Nikos, the watches are not Seikos. They are not stolen, but they are made in an Asian country, as are Seikos and, although they are not stolen, it is true that they arrived here without the usual duties being extorted."

"They are smuggled in from China?" I ventured.

"Exactly," Kostas replied then added, "They are of very good quality and very much like the brand name they carry. Do you think the Chinese would make a product so very different in quality than the Japanese, who are themselves only copying the Swiss?"

I had to concede the point.

"Nikos, do you think that the waiter, or the cheap prick at the table next to yours, care for more than what the label signifies? They don't care if the watch is as good as a Seiko, which it might be, only that people think that it is a Seiko, which people will. Nikos, you have made someone very happy today and you have made some money doing it. Rejoice!"

Over the next week, Kostas and I made a lot of money. In two weeks over the Christmas of 1969, I made more money than I had made teaching English in the previous three months. It got so that I could go up to a stranger in the street and unfold my pathetic story and come away three-hundred, sometimes five-hundred drachmas better off. Although, it must be said, the more I sold, the more rapidly the city shrank. Soon Kostas and I were taking the metro out to the suburbs.

The end, when it came, came suddenly, and right in the very centre of Athens. The place was an antique store in Constitution Square, on a street called Voulis Street. The store was called Techni, established in 1927, and owned by Stathis E. Kyrloglou. The interior of the store was dark as I came in from the afternoon sun. I went to the counter and the old man listened to my story and looked at the watch. His hair was white and the skin of his deeply creased face, mahogany. He went to his cash till and took out two thousand drachmas.

"I don't want your watch; it is a gift from your father. Take this and go to your girlfriend."

I tried to press the watch on him, but he was resolute, "I have no need of your watch. At my age time is my enemy and I have no need to be reminded of its passing. Take the money. It is my gift."

When I went out and met Kostas, I had a lump in my throat. "I can't do this anymore, Kostas, I'm finished. That old man believed my story. He wouldn't take the watch. He wasn't looking to make a gain. I'm finished, Kostas, I'm finished."

"Nikos, Nikos, slowly my friend, slowly, slowly. We are a great team, you and I. If I had a drachma for every old fool who'd bought a watch from me, why, I'd be a wealthy man."

But that was it for Kostas and me. I never sold a watch after that and only saw Kostas again a couple of times. The first time was a couple of months later. I was sitting at the outdoor café in the Museu Gardens reading a two-day-old copy of *The Sunday Times*. Kostas, wearing the same big jacket and accompanied by a young man of around my own age, walked over from the direction of the Polytechnio. I got up and we embraced as friends do. Kostas made the introductions. "Nikos, this is Claude, Claude, Nikos." I shook hands with the young man and we all three sat down.

"Claude is from Marseilles." Kostas said, adding, "He came to Athens hoping to teach French. Of course French is not so useful now."

"Let me guess," I said.

"Of course," Kostas replied, "What else."

The waiter appeared with my *café turkio* and Kostas ordered the same for himself and his new salesman.

"You and I were the best, Nikos."

"It was a good time, Kostas," I replied.

Two years later, I came back to Athens with my first wife and, although not blonde, she was in my eyes more beautiful than the girl in the picture. We went together to the store at Voulis Street. I had the two thousand drachmas in my pocket. There was a young man at the counter. "I'm sorry, Mr. Kyrloglou, my father, he passed away last year." I felt the heat behind my eyes and the rush in my throat. I turned abruptly and left the store with the two-thousand drachmas still in my pocket. I should have given it to his son, but I didn't. I felt too ashamed and, until I wrote this down, I had not forgiven myself.

A Place To Hang Out

"WHAT DO YOU SAY THEN, GEORGE'S IS IT?" The speaker, a thin boy with a thatch of parchment hair framing an unnaturally pale face, spoke without enthusiasm or inflection. His features were sharp and pinched, drained of character and emotion so that, although he didn't look older than his fifteen years, he did not resemble a child either. His face was a *tabula rasa* on which only disappointment, lack of love, and the certainty of failure had been written.

"Yeah, he'll have videos and shit, and we can have pizza," said the second boy. Known as Mouse to his friends, he was the younger by seven months. Although smaller than his friend and despite his youth, there was a wiry muscularity about him. His face sharp and alert, he could easily be mistaken for being the older of the two.

"Yeah," agreed the first boy whose full name was Richard Ian Norman Oats, and that was why, of course, he was known to his friends as Rhino. Rhino was excavating the contents of his left nostril as they walked. After examining the glistening result of his efforts, he flicked it to one side before continuing, "He's a funny fucker. I mean he's a perv, but he's all right, if you know what I mean."

"Fuck, Rhino," said the younger boy, "you got a fucking thing for him?"

"Fuck off, Mouse."

Mouse laughed abruptly. "You could do worse, Rhino. He's an old perv all right but, the thing is, he's an old perv with money. My old man had money, but he just pissed it down the pub. Having a heart attack was the only useful thing he ever fucking did for us, and that wasn't that much. My mum bought me a blazer from the pay out and we had four days at Long Beach. Can you believe that? What would I do with a fucking blazer, Rhino? And what can you fucking do at fucking Long Beach?" Mouse sniffed noisily then hawked up a long slick of phlegm onto the sidewalk. "If the old faggot gets his jollies getting me off, do I fucking care? I don't give a fuck as long as he's paying for pizza an' beer an' shit, and so long as he doesn't get any weird ideas about sticking his ol' one-eyed snake anywhere."

"Has he ever tried it?" asked Rhino, carefully, "I mean, sticking it . . . you know?"

Mouse looked across at his friend, "Are you fucking kidding, Rhino? I'd fucking kill the old fucker. He can jerk me off if that's what turns his crank. Like I said, I don't give a shit but if he ever tries that other shit, he's fucking dead, him an' his cat."

Mouse wore a thin hoodie and stovepipe blue jeans. He walked with a bow-legged, toes-out swagger. Rhino was wearing a beige corduroy shirt hanging outside of a pair of black nylon track pants and swaggered with less conviction than his friend. Mouse owned his swagger; Rhino looked like he was taking his for a test drive. Arriving at the corner of Garden Road and Carnation Street, the boys turned down toward George's house.

The area was subsidized housing — row upon row of identical units fronted by small strips of weedy lawn and desiccated privet. George's house was the exception. It was a house from another time. The casual onlooker might judge it possible that a long time ago, it had once been an imposing home, perhaps the home of a well-off industrialist or professional, and they would have been right. Now the wrought-iron gate was rusted, the pathway broken and weed-riven, and the paint, like the hinges, peeled away from the wooden shutters that flanked the windows. The property stood in damp and dishevelled dignity in the mottled shade cast by an ancient elm, an imposing, but decaying, pile fingered by death.

Many years earlier, the municipality had announced it intended to expropriate the large tract of land upon which the house and its then half-dozen neighbours stood to build subsidized housing. All, except George's father, had agreed to the terms of the buy-out. It was his home, he argued, where he had lived with his wife until her death during childbirth with George, and it was where he would die. George's father, a decorated veteran of WW2, who didn't take kindly to petty bureaucrats, had been resolute in resisting the forced purchase, and, in fact, had spent a good part of what might have been George's inheritance on that resistance. He had finally won the battle in Supreme Court, although the lawyers carried off the spoils, and when the old man died, he left George the house and not a lot more.

But, even before the old man's death, the same municipal council that had wanted to demolish the house, declared it a heritage building and, as such, it could be neither demolished nor altered. When the municipality informed the old man that his home had been thus designated and that he was entitled to a plaque for his front door bearing the legend, *A Heritage Building — The Maidstone Historical Society,* the feisty veteran had declined and, instead, fashioned his own very similar plaque which read, *An Old Dump — The Maidstone Hysterical Society.*

Thus it was that George, a machinist at Reynolds before the injury to his arm, resided in isolated splendour in what had been his childhood home, the only private homeowner in a quarter-mile radius, a reclusive, cardboard prince in his decaying, clapboard castle.

It was almost ten o'clock on a bright spring morning, when the two boys pushed open the front gate and made their way up the broken and uneven pathway. Had they bothered to go to school that morning, they would have just been completing their first class, Social Studies. As it happened, that was the only school subject that either boy had the slightest interest in attending, and that was solely because of the teacher, Sonia Lay. Sonia Lay's body, and the access to it suggested by her family name, was the cause of constant fantasizing among almost the entire male student body, and only a little less overtly, the male faculty.

"I wonder what the Lay's wearing today?" asked Mouse, voicing his fantasizing out loud without expecting any response.

"I'll bet she's wearing that see-through blouse that you can see her bra through," answered Rhino dreamily.

"Yeah. I could be up that like a rat up a fucking drain," said Mouse with bitter energy.

"Yeah, but she has a boyfriend, that dickhead that picks her up sometimes in the black Beamer," mused Rhino as he weighed the likelihood of his friend achieving his fantasy goal with Ms. Lay.

"Yeah, fucking pencil dick," retorted Mouse, dismissively, and then, "nice fucking wheels though, that Beemer."

"Yeah, fucking five-series, goes like shit," concurred Rhino.

The two youths climbed the broad steps that led up to the sagging porch which, in keeping with the rest of the property, reeked of age and neglect and boasted, among the miscellany of things that littered its length, a broken and sagging armchair, half-a-dozen cardboard boxes stuffed with long-playing records in mildewed covers, a metal standard lamp that hadn't worked in years, and an elaborate, but empty, multi-story white wire bird-cage with a rusting metal tray as its floor. The boys picked their way across to the double doors, then Mouse pulled open the unlocked right-hand door and the two stepped inside.

The interior was in semi-darkness even at this time of day, and smelt thickly of damp plaster and cat urine. A single, broad shaft of sunlight lanced across the hallway and a steady drift of dust fell across the illuminated air.

"What a dump," whispered Rhino.

"Hey, George! It's Mouse, Mouse and Rhino," Mouse called out, but in a lower voice to Rhino, "It's a fucking dump, Rhino, but the fucking council paid George's old man a fucking fortune to put in slum fucking housing all around it. My dad knew that kind of shit 'cause he worked for the council. He told my mum, and my mum told me that George's old man turned down fifty fucking 'g's', that's like a quarter mil now. Can you fucking believe that? George is worth a fucking fortune, the fuck, if his dad turned down a fuckin' quarter mil. Figure it, Rhino, if the fucker turned down that much, what the fuck did he accept, eh? Tell me that."

"I thought the old man turned down the money because that would have meant him moving and that's why George still has the house?" said Rhino uncertainly.

"Use your fucking head, Rhino. No one turns down that kind of money to stay in a dump like this," said Mouse confidently. "Take it from me, Rhino, the ol' fucker's worth a fucking mint."

At the first sound of the voice, the cat, Felix, had leapt from the shadows, bolted across the hall, and shot up the stairs. Mouse's Doc Martins had, too often, abruptly and violently abbreviated the cat's afternoon nap for it to delay its exit.

"Fucking cat," said Mouse, "My mother used to have a cat, a fucking evil thing, fucking Siamese or some shit with big fuckin' blue eyes. I hated that fucking cat, the way it used to look at me; gave me the fucking creeps. I think she fucking liked that cat more than me." Then, suddenly, Mouse gave a high-pitched laugh. "Ha, ha, ha, I fucking nailed that bastard — ha, ha, ha — you should of fuckin' seen it, fuckin' lit it up with lighter fuel. It went up like a fuckin' bonfire, all its fucking hair on fire. It didn't know whether to shit or run in circles. I guess it did both. I near pissed myself laughing. My mum was all broke up, went on and on about what kind of sick fuck would do such a thing. I told her I thought it was some Paki kids. That really rattled her cage. She didn't like those fuckers to start with. We even had a funeral for it. Can you believe that? A funeral for a cat." Mouse smiled at the memory. "I wrote a poem for my mum. It was pretty good. Hey, not that I'm into fucking poetry, Rhino, fuck that. My mother cried when she read it, she was all over me. I teared up myself to tell you the truth, well, I mean, seeing my mum all crying and stuff. Said she knew I was upset and shit, and writing it down would help bring it out. Bring what out? I didn't know what the fuck she was talking about. She said maybe I was going to be a writer, how she'd knew all along that I was smart, and how my dad was an asshole." Mouse paused to reflect on this last comment, then added, "Which he no doubt was."

"Hello, boys." George emerged from out of the gloom of the hallway. His greeting had a sibilant quality to it, somewhere between a smoker's rasp and asthma although, in fact, George was neither a smoker nor an asthmatic.

"That was a lovely story, Mouse, and here's me thinking you hadn't a mean bone in your body. What a little minx you can be." George smiled slyly, before adding, "I certainly hope your mother never finds out."

"What's a minx, George?" asked Rhino.

"No way, George, she's totally convinced it's the Pakis," bragged Mouse, oblivious to any sinister inference that might be read into the older man's observation. "Fuck, I almost believe it myself sometimes. That's the kind of shit that those Pakis do, they eat cats and dogs like we eat chicken, those sick fuckers," he concluded.

"I think that's the Koreans and the Chinese but, no matter, you may well be right, and a minx is a sly little creature, Rhino," said George mildly.

George Bedwell was a man in his late forties, or maybe early fifties, it was hard to say. He was past his prime in any event. Over six feet tall and quite spare, he walked with a stoop, the result of a childhood during which, always taller than his classmates, he'd attempted to blend in by reducing his height by stooping. The habit had never left him and his upper spine was permanently accommodated to this posture.

Thinning brown hair curled over his ears, dandruff speckled the shoulders of his beige wool cardigan, and his plain grey pants looked slept in. "Anyway, come on in boys, come on in. I always enjoy young company," George said as he turned and led the way back into the living room, his slippered feet shuffling on carpet that hadn't seen shampoo in a decade.

Mouse turned toward Rhino and smirked.

Rhino smirked back.

The large living room into which George led them was furnished with both genuine antique and some merely old furnishings, and was dominated by three large, well-used, leather-covered easy chairs and a fabric-covered sofa. These were arranged in such a way that the focus of interest was clearly the large-screen television that stood like a black hole in one corner of the room. At ease in the house, Mouse flopped down in the nearest chair, the one with the TV remote resting on its broad arm.

"You working this afternoon, George?" asked Mouse, hitting the power button while staring at the yet dark screen.

George was already heading toward the kitchen for pop and corn chips with Rhino following. The television hissed briefly before the screen burst into noisy life.

"No, not today, Mouse," replied George without looking back. After the accident at Reynolds, George had won a healthy damages suit against the company, which, even after the lawyers had taken a hefty bite, when coupled with the little inheritance from his father, left him comfortable in his frugal lifestyle. He'd been on permanent disability since the accident even though any impairment was now so slight that it wasn't obvious there had been any injury at all. In fact, it was only during his annual Workers' Compensation Board check-ups that limitation in movement became pronounced.

Along with his payments from the WCB, George had also scored a little cash-under-the-table job at his accountant's house. It paid under minimum, but then it involved less than minimum effort — washing the three cars, keeping the grounds clean, and doing the odd bit of mending. He worked one weekday morning and one afternoon. It wasn't heavy work and it got him out of the house. With little to spend his money on, his weekly food bill was barely more than the cat's, and he bought clothes only when something finally disintegrated. George found that most weeks his WCB payments stayed in his bank. Today though, was a Thursday and one of his days off. "I thought I'd just kick back, chill out, is that how you boys say it? Just stay around the house," George's voice carried from the kitchen.

Mouse could hear George opening cupboards and then the doors of the big double-door refrigerator. Then he heard George say something to Rhino that Mouse couldn't make out and it was followed by George's little high-pitched giggle. *Fucking George, priming Rhino for a bit of the other,* thought Mouse. Mouse knew exactly what George wanted to do this afternoon, and if George was going to be a part of it then he wanted to be sure there was something in it. Leaving the chair, Mouse dropped down onto his knees beside the big console that held the television and video-recorder. Pulling open the doors to the long cupboard at the base of the consul, he was confronted with the spines of around sixty video cassettes. Mixed in with titles such as *Star Wars, The Sound of Music,* and *Amadeus* were cassettes with less well-known titles such as *The Lay Over, David and Goliath,* and *Boys will be Boys.* Mouse selected a cassette entitled, *Maid Service,* slid the cassette into the VCR, returned to his chair and, picking up the remote, hit play. Mouse called out to his friend. "What do you say, Rhino, you want to come over to my place for a bite? My mum'll be gone or ... unless ... George, you making lunch later?"

George was used to the little negotiation that was always a part of dealing with Mouse. George allowed himself a bleak smile, reflecting that *the wretched child* always liked to know what he was getting before he went any further. "Oh, I don't know, I think I've got two or three little steaks in the freezer. I was just going to have one myself and maybe a beer. You know, the frugal repast of a lonely old man on a pension. You can probably do better than that at home — well, perhaps not the beer, but I'm sure your mother will have left you something tasty in the fridge," George concluded on a cheerful note while he pursued a line of thought closer to his true nature. *What hope of that, you little prick, with that tart you've got for a mother?*

It really pissed Mouse off when George came out with shit like that. *The fucker knew his mother was never home.*

With the opening credits starting to roll, the film began with a well-dressed woman of about thirty getting out of a car. She was wearing a short black skirt with a small slit in the side, had great legs, and was toting a carrier-style, shoulder bag.

She hadn't been home when his dad was alive, mostly because she couldn't stand his dad, and she hadn't been home since he died mostly because she was busy *trying to get fucking laid* by all his old workmates at the fucking Legion.

The woman pressed the bell of a pricey looking apartment building. The camera focused on her fingers, which were beautiful with perfect long red fingernails then, while she waited for the door to be answered, the lens trailed across her

different parts: her perfect ear lobe, the corner of her mouth,
where her nipple pricked at the soft material of her blouse.

While his libidinous brain remained riveted to the screen,
Mouse continued to brood on the matter of his mother. The
fuckin' Legion, the Viagra-veterans, and talk about mutton
dressed as fuckin' lamb. Fuck, she was almost forty and went
out looking like a fucking tart five nights a week. And the
fucks she brought back? They were either fucking drunks or
looked like they should have been on life-support. Something
tasty? Fuck! If she'd left anything in the fridge for him, it
would be *in a fuckin' can.* "So you're saying we're having steak
for lunch, George?" Mouse called through to the kitchen.

"Well I thought you were thinking of going back to your
place, Mouse?" George replied innocently, then said to Rhino,
"Here, Rhino, take these through for me, will you? There's
a good boy." As Rhino came into the room, eyes already
fastened to the screen, George's voice came after him, "Rhino,
what do you want to do?"

Setting down a bowl of corn chips and another of salsa,
Rhino looked toward Mouse. "Mouse?"

An older, distinguished-looking man with silver hair opened
the door and stood to one side to let the blonde woman
enter. He wasn't wearing regular clothes, but some sort of
housecoat. The scene then shifted to the plush interior of the
apartment. The man sat down on a long sofa and watched
the woman while she removed her jacket.

"Fucking jugs on that, eh, Rhino?" Mouse shifted uncom-
fortably in the chair as his libido responded to the images on
the screen. Although he'd first ignored the question, Mouse
had heard his friend. Now, while he stared intently at the
screen, he hissed, "Fuck, Rhino, think for your fuckin' self,

man." Then more softly he said, "Rhino, what do you want, man? You know what's going to fucking happen; just don't let him stick it up your ass."

Rhino didn't really have to think about the answer to that. He knew what George wanted to do. Fuck, it wasn't so bad. Rhino had never known his mother. She had left him before his memory started. He'd stayed with his dad, but hadn't seen much of him either. The only women he'd ever known had been the string of nameless women that threaded through his father's life. One had seemed to care for him for a while. He had a hazy recollection of a woman with ginger hair who used to read to him and take him to school. She read him *Peter Pan*. That was the only book he ever remembered being read to him. The only book he could remember from his childhood. He thought the woman's name might have been Ruth, or maybe Sarah — it had an 'h' in it anyway. There were others after her, but he couldn't remember any of them clearly. He couldn't remember ever being loved, or kissed, or held, or hardly ever touched. Nothing like his friends' parents were with their children. Sometimes, in the school playground, he'd stand and watch parents saying goodbye to their kids, picking them up and kissing them — some would even walk their kids into the school, all the way to the classroom, like they were something special, which they definitely weren't. He had other memories too, but they weren't good ones, and he'd spent so long trying not to remember that now it was like trying to see the detail of a shadow play glimpsed through a veil in a shaded room. Maybe the memories weren't even real.

"Fuck, Mouse, it's no big deal. You said so yourself, George is okay."

Now the woman was kneeling between the old man's legs.

Both boys watched in disbelief. Absentmindedly, Rhino put his finger in his mouth as far as he could and gagged immediately.

"Look at the size of his fucking cock," said Mouse, "It's bigger than my fucking arm."

"Well, boys, I see you've made yourselves at home and that you've found something edifying to watch," George said as he re-entered the room carrying with him three bottles of cream soda that he placed on the low coffee table.

"What?" replied Mouse.

"I said, I see you've found something horny to watch. Mouse, you must have missed *Sound of Music*. I have that too, you know."

"Yeah, whatever, George," replied Mouse staring intently at the screen.

George sat down on the sofa beside Rhino. "I see the film's got your interest too, Rhino," said George smiling, and looking at the crotch of Rhino's thin track pants. "You don't have to be shy on my account. It's only natural, you know. It's the way God made us, the way God planned it," George said, laying his hand on Rhino's knee.

Rhino didn't attempt to move the older man's hand. Mouse was right; he knew what was going to happen, and it wasn't like he really minded; George liked him.

Mouse picked up one of the sodas and took a long pull from the bottle, the beads of cold condensation running down over the web of skin between his thumb and forefinger. He looked across at his friend, and at George's hand hooked like a talon across the top of Rhino's thigh.

After lunch with George, they'd remained watching pornography and an old Clint Eastwood spaghetti western throughout the afternoon. Around 5:00, George had sent Mouse out for pizza. With Mouse not two minutes out of the door, George stood in front of a kneeling Rhino, the boy's head clamped between his large hands.

"Come on, Rhino . . . there's a good boy, and you make sure you swallow now, none of that spitting it out stuff," ordered George.

Over at the pizza store, sitting in a chair with an ice-cold coke in his hand, flicking over the pages of *People* magazine and waiting while the pizza baked in the big oven, Mouse smiled. He could well imagine what was happening back at George's place. It wasn't like it hadn't happened before — it had.

Fuck! That Brad Pitt was a lucky fucker, fucking that Jennifer Aniston babe — she hardly wore any fucking clothes. Imagine coming home to that every night. Mouse turned the page to Jennifer Lopez. *Holy shit! Look at the tits on that*, thought Mouse.

The first time had been an evening when George had given them more than a few beers. Mouse couldn't remember everything that had happened, but he remembered bits. He remembered bits of a movie, a little Asian girl getting the hammer from a big fat Indian looking guy and George's hand on his dick, jerking him off. He remembered throwing up in the bathroom, bits of pizza, the rank stench of vomit, and stale beer. He remembered George kneeling in front of Rhino, his narrow head with its thinning, wispy brown hair bobbing up and down. Mouse had watched from the doorway to the bathroom. *Fuck, Rhino was right into it, fucking groaning and moaning and calling for his fucking mummy, the stupid fuck. She ditched you, buddy, fuck!* There had been a few times after that as well. On one of these occasions, George had again sent Mouse out for pizza. Mouse, however, had crept back in and listened outside the living room door. He could hear low voices, then a lot of grunting and groaning, George's voice all angry and harsh calling Rhino a bitch, and Rhino crying out. After they left he asked Rhino what had happened, but Rhino just said "fuck all," *the lying bastard*. After that, Mouse had come to believe that George was, in fact, *an evil old fucker*, but nevertheless it was a good place to hang out.

It was after one of these evenings at the house that Mouse had again raised the issue of George's undoubted wealth.

"I'm telling you, man, he's got money. You see his wallet when he pulled off that twenty? I'm telling you, man, he's fucking loaded," Mouse said. "I'll bet he keeps a big fucking stash 'round the place somewhere."

"No one keeps money 'round the house, Mouse. He'll have it in the bank," replied Rhino.

Rhino had a memory of a bank, with his father, the Dominion Bank, on the corner of a street, watching from a bus. A black man walked in, his father looked over and said, "There goes another coon, depositing his welfare cheque." Rhino recognized the man; it was his friend Cecil's father, Nelson, who'd always been good to him. Sometimes Rhino had waited at Cec's house, to walk with him to school. Nelson had made the boys breakfast a couple of times and somehow seemed to know that Rhino never got breakfast at home. After that, Rhino used to arrive early two or three times a week, and for almost a whole school year the breakfasts with Cec and his family were the only ones he ever had. Then Nelson bought a house in the suburbs, and Rhino only saw Cec a couple more times after that. The last time was more

than a couple of years ago. Rhino knew, too, that Nelson was
a bus driver and that his wife, Winnie, was a night nurse at
the big hospital in the city centre, and they'd probably never
pulled welfare in their life. But he was too embarrassed to say
anything to his dad, who he knew was *full of shit.*

"In the bank? Are you fucking kidding? Have you ever
seen the fucker outside? He's like a fucking ghost, man. He
hardly ever goes further than the store on the corner, unless
it's for beer. I'm telling you, man, he's never short of cash and
I'll bet there's a big fat, fucking stash right under his bed or
someplace fucking obvious."

"You think so, Mouse? You think so?" said Rhino

"What the fuck, Rhino, of course I don't fucking think so,
I fucking know so."

It was shortly after that conversation that Mouse had
come out with his plan. As Mouse saw it, it was simple. It was
a given that there was a stash of money in the house. Mouse
stated that with the same certainty as if he'd said the world is
round, or if you let go of something, it will fall to the ground
and not fly upwards. There were two ways to get to George's
stash: they could go in the house when George was out, which
was hardly ever; or, find a way to check out the house during
the many times they were over there.

"Rhino," began Mouse, "you remember that last time
at George's when I went to get the pizza and left you with
George?"

"Yeah," said Rhino

"Well, I didn't go straight away; I came back inside," said
Mouse.

"Yeah," said Rhino again, more slowly.

"Well, I saw old George give it to you in the ass," Mouse said, feeling quite certain from what he had heard through the door that that was exactly what had happened.

"Bullshit, man, that's bullshit," blustered Rhino angrily.

"Hey, man, don't worry. I'm not going to say anything. Don't fucking worry," Mouse assured his friend.

"There's nothing to say, Mouse. That's bullshit, man," repeated Rhino, but without even the pretend passion this second time.

"Hey, look man, I don't give a shit. We've both done stuff with him — that's not the fucking point. The thing is, while he was doing whatever it was he wasn't fucking doing, I could have gone through the whole fucking place. You with me?"

"I never took it up the ass, man," said Rhino quietly.

"Hey, whatever the fuck, Rhino. Are you fucking listening? Are you getting the fucking picture, man?" Mouse retorted impatiently.

"Yeah, I think so," said Rhino slowly, then after a moment he added, "but he'll know it was us, Mouse."

"Yeah, and what's he gonna do Rhino? Complain to the cops that some kids he's been fucking with ripped him off? He can't do nothing man; he'll just have to fucking suck it up. Anyway, we won't take it all — I'm not greedy — we'll take just enough."

So that was the plan. Nothing too complicated. Rhino would keep George occupied while Mouse, who ostensibly had gone out to get the pizza, would be checking out the house and ripping off George's stash.

After leaving school mid-afternoon less than a week later, the two boys once again wound their way over to George's place.

"Come on in, boys, so nice to see you again," said George. "Are you here for a visit, to keep an old man company, or just passing through?" George smiled, then added solicitously, "I hope your poor mother isn't waiting at home for you, Mouse with a nice hot meal, worrying where you are."

"Yeah, right, George," Mouse snapped, angering quickly at George's habitual chafing. *I'll fucking enjoy ripping you off you fuck,* he thought.

Rhino didn't say anything, but slumped down at the end of the sofa nearest the television. Mouse sorted through the videos until he came up with *Smartie Pants* and slid it into the VCR. Meanwhile, George had gone to the kitchen and returned with three beers and a bag of chips, putting them down on the antique rosewood coffee table with ornate claw feet. The two boys had taken the sofa, so George sat down in the chair closest to Mouse, smiling fondly as he watched the boys watching the movie and sucking back their beer. George took the occasional sip of his. The film followed the same old routine. The boys had seen it before, but were riveted to the screen nevertheless — at least until halfway through when Mouse, suddenly restless, announced, "That was fucking good pizza we had last time, George."

"It wasn't what I asked for, Mouse. I told you what to get," said George with some irritation.

"I don't like all that vegetable stuff," Mouse replied a little petulantly

"That's why you're always hungry, Mouse, you don't eat proper food. I don't wonder you don't put on any weight," George said. And, while encircling Mouse's upper arm with his thumb and forefinger, he added reprovingly, "Tsk, tsk, tsk, skin and bone, skin and bone — you need fattening up." Then, sitting forward, George leaned over to one side and slid his wallet out from his back pocket. Pulling out a wad of notes, he peeled off a twenty and handed it to Mouse. "But I want Greek, Mouse," he said harshly, "not that pineapple and cheese crap that you got last time."

"All right, George, no worries. You'll get Greek for sure, eh Rhino?" Mouse smirked at Rhino, his back to George as he rose from the sofa.

"I dunno, maybe I'll . . . " Rhino started to get up from the chair.

"No, man, you stay here and watch the end of the movie. See how the fucking plot develops," Mouse said sharply.

"That's right, Rhino, you stay and keep old George company. Tell me what's going on in your young lives."

Mouse grinned from the doorway. "Yeah, Rhino, I won't be long. Back in half an hour." Then, slamming the door behind him, Mouse made a great play of stamping across the porch.

George got to his feet and walked into the kitchen. Pulling open the fridge, he brought out two more beers, then walked back into the living area where Rhino had become absorbed in the goings on of two young undergraduate students and their professor. George placed the beers on the table, then sank down on the sofa next to Rhino. Almost immediately, he placed his hand on Rhino's crotch.

"Why, Rhino, you're excited already and those naughty girls have hardly got started. I think you're going to need some help." George reached across, and slid his hand in under the waist of Rhino's track pants.

Rhino didn't react, but sat there staring at the screen, where the young professor sat at his desk, legs apart and spectacles askew while the two young students, naked from the waist up, knelt between his legs.

"What would you like, Rhino, what would you like me to do to make to make you feel better?" asked George.

"Call me Ricky, will you George? Call me Ricky," said Rhino softly, still glued to the television.

George smiled, "Sure I will, Rhino. Ricky it is. So who used to call you that, who used to call you Ricky?" asked George. "Is that what your dad used to call you?"

Rhino shook his head. "I don't remember."

George wanted to laugh, but instead continued to smile, a tender, compassionate, smile. *You pathetic, fucked up little shit,* he thought. "You just come to Georgie, Ricky. You just come to Georgie," said George and, turning on the sofa, lowered his head into Rhino's lap. He couldn't see Rhino's face, or the tears beneath the boy's closed eyelids.

Upstairs, Mouse was already frustrated. He had been through the bedroom and found nothing. He'd checked under the bed, the mattress, the back of the drawers, under the sweaters — not a thing. All he'd found were dildos, lubricants, and porno magazines. *Where the fuck would the old fuck keep a quarter million dollars or whatever the fuck?* Mouse kicked the chest of drawers that he had just looked through, then recoiled at the noise he'd made. "Fuck!"

Mouse needn't have worried; downstairs in the living room the two girls on the screen were moaning and screaming while George's head was bobbing rapidly over Rhino's groin. The youth moaned quietly, his tears now dirty tracks across his cheeks. Neither heard a sound from the upstairs bedroom.

There were three bedrooms, but the other two were so crammed with junk that the prospect of searching them was daunting. Mouse crept back down the stairs and, at the bottom, glanced at the carriage clock that stood on the table in the hall. Ten minutes had passed already. "Shit," Mouse whispered. He looked at the closed door to the living room. He was tempted to cross over and listen again, but the thought of the money dissuaded him. He tried to put himself in George's shoes. If not the bedroom, which, upon reflection, now seemed too obvious, where? Mouse decided that the small room that George called his study was a likely spot. Carefully avoiding the creaking floorboard, he tiptoed quietly across the hallway, past the door to the living room, and opened the door into the study.

Although he'd been in the room before, Mouse had not taken much interest. Pushing the door quietly closed behind him, he looked at the contents of the room. It was not surprising that the air was thick with the odour of old damp paper. One wall was lined with books end to end and floor to ceiling. There were boxes of books, slumping piles of *National Geographic*s, and stacks of magazines slewed over into untidy heaps. George had told the boys that his old man was a garage sale freak, and that's where all this stuff had come from. The second, much shorter, wall had a window in it. A large oak desk abutted the wall, the top littered with what looked like bills in sepia envelopes — many unopened — and piles of assorted papers and folders.

At the back of the desktop was a black and white portrait of a man in military uniform — army, Mouse guessed from the shade of the uniform, and leather holster. Another picture was of that same man and a small woman who wore a flowing hat and was obviously pregnant. Mouse figured that it was George's parents. "Fuck it," said Mouse softly. He pulled open the shallow middle drawer of the desk. It was full of more old bills, ball-point pens, pencils, rubber bands, paper clips, note pads, a couple of diaries, assorted keys and key rings, screws, and anonymous bits of metal. There were six more drawers, three to a side. Mouse quickly looked through them, at least until he came to the last, which, unlike the other five, was locked. *Fuck. I fucking knew it, the old fuck.* He looked around for something with which he might pry the drawer open. Nothing. He shuffled the papers around on the top of the desk — he knew he'd seen something when he first came in the room, something hovering just off in the wings of his memory. Then he saw it, a long, thin, silver letter opener. He grabbed it and, kneeling down in front of the desk, jammed it into the top of the drawer. The opener bent to a thirty-five degree angle but the drawer stayed shut. "Fuck. Fuck." Mouse knew that he was running out of time. He looked at the misshapen opener. Placing the opener on the floor, Mouse stood on it. It still wasn't straight. He took it between his hands and bent it some more. Now, it seemed rippled in the middle. "Fucking thing!" Mouse muttered, and threw the opener across the room. It thudded, quivering, stuck, at chest height, in the door frame.

Mouse looked around the room again; there was nothing else that he could use. Then he remembered the handful of keys in the middle drawer. Gathering up several loose keys, he placed them on the floor, then knelt before the locked drawer. He worked his way through the collection of keys and was down to the last two when a bronze key that looked far too big, nonetheless, did the trick. The drawer was stiff. Wiggling it open gently and quietly was going nowhere, or if not nowhere, then not quickly enough for Mouse in his increasing agitation. He gave the drawer a violent wrench. There was the shriek of wood upon wood, and the drawer stood open halfway. Mouse looked inside. "Holy shit."

Across the hall, behind the closed door of the living room, Rhino was bent forward across the broad arm of the sofa, his hands gripping the cushions. He was uttering short grunts of what might have been pain or pleasure as George, indifferent to which, stood against the child's buttocks, eyes closed, mouth open, forcing his way into him. Then George froze. Even above the pounding of his blood and the wretched boy's whimpering, the sudden sound, a sound that came from within the house was unmistakable. George was not oblivious to the socially and legally unacceptable character of his preference for young boys as sexual partners. That he should consider society wrong, didn't blind him to the fact that society would punish him for his preference if it could. The knock on the door, the "Are you Mr. George Baldwin?" from some clean-cut young cop's mouth was a nightmare that he knew would one day happen. It had happened already. *It wasn't fair,* George screamed in his head. He didn't ask to feel like this; it was who he was.

He remembered the first time he'd been placed on probation — that's what they called it, being placed on probation. The young probation officer was a girl, really, a young blonde girl who, he had quickly discovered was too naïve to keep her personal life to herself, had a cop for a fiancée. She had to boast about her normality, her plans to marry, to have two children. George remembered her asking him about taking treatment. Treatment? Treatment for what? What did she think it was that he had, the measles? What did she think he was, a lab specimen? George knew what he was, he was a homosexual hebephile. He'd read the books. Did they think he could be treated into heterosexuality? Could she be treated into homosexual hebephelia, he'd asked her. The silly little bitch, she couldn't even make sense of the question. Talk about lack of imagination. Had she even looked at the classics? Was her idea of an education a social work degree? The noise from within his home, the noise that he had distinctly heard, brought all these thoughts flooding to the forefront of his consciousness. "Shut up, Rhino," George hissed.

"What, Daddy, what?" asked Rhino, plaintively.

George, his face a mask of contempt, looked down at the boy. The boy's thin back, the knotted worm of his spine, the pale spotty blossoms of his buttocks. This wretched creature was going to cause him untold misery. At any moment the door would burst open, the cops would rush in, disgust and seething hatred on their faces. He'd be beaten to the floor, handcuffed, read his rights. In those few seconds, as his head stormed with such visions, George's cock withered. He quickly withdrew, pushing his clothes into his pants, then leaning forward, his face close to Rhino's ear, he said in an acid voice, "I'm not your daddy, Rhino, you dumb little fuck. Now shut the fuck up."

Mouse looked at his find. Money to be sure, an envelope stuffed with twenties. He riffled through the notes, a couple of hundred bucks easy, a nice score, although where was the big money? But of more interest was the bulky, deep-brown leather holster and the grey, steel butt of the gun that it contained. Mouse put the envelope down and reached into the drawer, closed his fingers over the holster, and brought it out. He held it between his hands. "Fuck," said Mouse out loud. The weight surprised him. He'd had no idea guns were so heavy. He snapped open the holster and removed the revolver. The chambers were empty. He looked back into the drawer but there was nothing — no bullets. Then he remembered something. He re-opened the middle drawer and saw the two, small, brown cardboard boxes. He had ignored them before because they could not possibly hold money, and the ".38" stamped on them had meant nothing to him. Now, it was different. He picked up one of the boxes, held it in his left hand and, with his right, levered open the tight brown top. The bases of twenty-four rounds of tightly packed .38 calibre bullets ran in four rows the length of the box. Mouse plucked one out and felt the focused weight of it in his palm.

Some moments had passed since the squeal of the reluctant drawer had interrupted George. He had moved back from where he'd been standing between Rhino's thighs, and was listening intently. Perhaps he'd been mistaken. Could he hear something else?

"What's up Geo . . . " started Rhino.

"Shut up, Rhino," repeated George, although less harshly now that the immediate fear of discovery had begun to abate, "and put your pants on, Ricky. There's a good boy. I'll be back in a moment."

"Where . . . ?" Rhino began, already clambering clumsily back into his clothes.

"Shush," said George

One by one, Mouse removed six cartridges from the box and slid them into the waiting chambers of the revolver. With the last one filled, Mouse snapped the .38 Smith & Wesson standard military issue revolver back together.

"Pow! Pow! Pow!" Mouse aimed the gun at different targets around the room, stiff-armed, both hands on the handle of the gun, finger on the trigger — like he'd seen the cops do on television. Then he stood motionless, staring through the narrow opening in the curtains, to the street outside. Seeing the occasional car hiss by in the light drizzle, he wondered what it would feel like to blow some completely unsuspecting dumb fucker away.

"That little thieving fucker," whispered George, from his position crouched down outside the study door, right eye up against the ancient keyhole. He could see the desk with a couple of drawers open, including the one he kept locked. His last week's payment from his caretaker's job for the accountant, who always paid in cash, was strewn across the carpet by the desk. Mouse stood with his back to him, staring out of the window. George threw open the door and started into the room, "You thieving little shit . . . oh, ooh!"

Mouse didn't even think. It was not even like it was him that did it. One moment he'd been fantasizing about blowing away some motorist, the next, still half in the fantasy, he'd whirled and pulled the trigger, twice, like he'd seen on a thousand cop shows, without even really forming the intent to do so. Fantasy melded into reality in one blistering, irrevocable instant. He heard and saw George speak but, in the same compressed moment, George seemed to fly backwards with his chest and face exploding.

The sound of the two rapid explosions filled the air in the small room, echoing and reverberating until all that was left was a shocked stillness, burnt air, and a tiny sucking noise from George who lay like a broken doll, torso in the hallway, legs splayed out in the study.

Mouse stood in shocked disbelief, not at what he'd done — he couldn't yet make that connection — but simply at what had happened. He was still gripping the gun with both hands, although he'd let his stiff arms fall slowly down so that the weapon pointed to the floor. Mouse became aware that another figure was standing just beyond the doorway.

"Holy fucking shit, Mouse. Holy fucking shit. What have you fucking done?" Rhino whispered, his hands gripping the top of his hastily pulled-up track pants.

Mouse looked up beyond the mess that was welling up around George's shattered head and torso. He didn't speak, but continued to stand there staring at his friend, then down at George's body until finally, still looking at George, he said softly, "Did you fucking see that, Rhino? Did you fucking see that? Did you see the way his fucking head blew apart? Did you see what I did, Rhino. Did you see what I did? Mouse started to laugh, slowly at first, then in a high-pitched giggle.

"What are we going to do, Mouse?" said Rhino, his eyes fixed on George's broken body. "You've killed George. What are we going to do, Mouse?"

Mouse brought his giggling under control. Lowering himself slowly to a squatting position, he laid the gun down on the floor beside him and, leaning forward, started to pick up the scattered bank notes. He paused and looked up thoughtfully at Rhino, "It's like I said, Rhino, the old perv had it coming. He was an evil bastard. He was abusing us. We're just kids." Mouse looked at the wad of notes in his hand. "We'll split this fifty-fifty, Rhino, even though I did the shooting."

Acknowledgements

Thanks to my friends in the writing community who have been so generous of their time, and merciless in their honesty. Thanks also to Thistledown Press for taking a chance on a new author and whose editorial commentary, makes 'merciless' read like tender-hearted.

NICK FARAGHER has lived and travelled in many different countries including Greece, Italy, and France. These particular locales inform and inspire the fiction in this first collection. His writing also draws on his employment in probation and parole, where he prepared personality profiles on offenders in every category of crime but, specifically, on those offenders with psychiatric disorders as well as those guilty of offences of a sexual nature. Faragher has written articles for national, provincial and local magazines and newspapers. He currently lives with his partner, Donelda, on a sailboat usually moored at a small island in BC's Georgia Straight.